Natasha

Natasha's Badge
Natasha's Swing
Natasha the Brownie

Veronica Heley
Illustrated by Annabel Large

Scripture Union
130 City Road, London EC1V 2NJ

By the same author

Natasha's Dare

Tiger Books
Good for Kate!
Dancing Feet

Leopard Books
Hawkeye of Paradise Row
The Paradise Row Gang
Hawkeye hits the Jackpot

Swift Books
Sky High

Impressions
Penguin Theatre

© Veronica Heley 1986 – Natasha's Badge
© Veronica Heley 1987 – Natasha's Swing
© Veronica Heley 1990 – Natasha the Brownie

First published as combined edition 1992
© Veronica Heley 1992

ISBN 0 86201 805 6

British Library Cataloguing-in-Publication Data.
A catalogue record for this book is available from the British Library.

Phototypeset by Intype, London
Printed and bound in Great Britain by
Cox and Wyman Ltd Reading

NATASHA'S BADGE

Contents

Fish friends

Natasha was in trouble.

'I can't help it,' said Natasha. 'My mug slipped and emptied milk all over me.'

'What am I going to do with you?' asked her mother. 'It's such hard work keeping you clean and tidy. I've never known a girl like you for losing things and getting yourself dirty.'

'Accidents just seem to happen to me,' said Natasha, unhappily.

'It will be a long time before we buy you a fish badge, if you go on like this.'

Natasha did want a fish badge so badly! Her Sunday School teacher wore one and so did her mother and father. Natasha wanted one not only because it was pretty, but because it would show everyone that she loved Jesus. One of her favourite games was playing at being an early Christian, hiding from the soldiers in the caves and tunnels under Rome, and chalking the fish sign on the walls to show which way you'd gone. Just like the very first Christians.

But it didn't look as if she would be getting her fish very soon.

She made lots of good resolutions about keeping clean and tidy as she went off to school. When she came to the house where the large black dog lived, she crossed over and walked on the opposite side of the road. It wasn't that she was afraid, exactly, but she didn't care for dogs that growled at you, even when you weren't the kind of girl who teased them.

Usually a nice friendly girl sat beside Natasha in class, but today that girl had measles, and the teacher put a new boy there instead.

Natasha didn't have anything against boys. They could climb and swim and jump almost as well as she could. But this boy was small and pale and altogether beneath her notice.

The teacher asked the new boy to spell his name, which was long and didn't sound English. The new boy spoke in a growly voice, and everyone laughed. The teacher said she'd call him Pod for short and everyone laughed again. Natasha laughed, too, even though she could see it made the new boy feel uncomfortable.

He followed her around the playground at break, until she told him to go away.

'But I don't know anyone,' he said, in his growly voice.

'So what?' said Natasha rudely, and turned her back on him to talk to one of her friends.

Now Natasha wasn't usually unkind, and it bothered her when she thought about how small Pod was. There were a couple of big boys in the class who liked to bully newcomers, and Natasha had a feeling they'd soon find Pod and make trouble for him.

She looked round and sure enough, the two bullies had got Pod up against the wall and were pushing and shoving him. Pod wasn't crying, but he didn't look happy.

Natasha thought, Well, it's not my business to keep him out of trouble. He's a complete stranger.

Then she saw that Pod was wearing a tiny golden fish on his blazer, and that changed everything. The fish was exactly like the ones her father and mother wore, and if Pod were a Christian, too, then he wasn't a stranger, but a sort of brother.

She pushed into the circle around Pod and said, 'You leave him alone. He's my friend!'

'You keep out of this!' said the largest boy,

and he gave Natasha such a push that she fell
over in the mud.

Someone gave a piercing whistle.

'Watch it!' said the second boy, and they
melted away as one of the teachers walked past.

'Was that you whistling?' said Natasha to
Pod. 'I wish I could whistle like that. Will you
teach me?'

'Sure,' he said. 'And thanks for helping me
out. Of course, I wasn't really frightened.'

'Of course not,' said Natasha, being polite.

Pod helped Natasha to dust herself down,
and that afternoon he helped her with her
number work. He was brilliant at numbers. He
found her hair-ribbon when it dropped off, and
she shared her sandwiches with him at lunch-
time because he hadn't brought any of his own.

They walked home together, because it
turned out that Pod had come to live with his
mother in a flat above the shops at the top of
Natasha's road. Natasha was so busy telling
Pod about her family and friends and the
Sunday School outing next month, and how
her mother had promised to buy her a fish
badge, that she forgot all about the dog. She
nearly fell over him, and of course he growled
and showed his teeth.

'Oh!' she screamed.

The dog growled again.

'Hello, you great big dog, you!' said Pod, and actually stopped to have a chat with him. The dog sniffed all over Pod's outstretched hand, and then licked it.

Natasha walked round the dog and waited for Pod to join her.

'We had a dog once,' said Pod. 'Dogs all seem to like me.'

'I wasn't really frightened,' said Natasha. 'Just surprised.'

Pod smiled. 'We're fish friends, aren't we? We help one another, right?'

'Right!' said Natasha.

The hungry ones

Natasha was worried about Pod. He'd been coming to their school for a whole week now, and he hadn't yet brought any food for his lunch. He hadn't brought any dinner money, either. Some children brought money on Mondays and gave it to the teacher, who booked them in to have meals in the school hall. But not Pod.

Natasha wasn't greedy. She didn't mind sharing her sandwiches with Pod, but Pod still looked starved when he'd eaten half her food, and she was getting hollow places in her tummy long before tea-time, because she quite liked food, herself.

Natasha's mother had a part-time job at the garden centre up the road, and every morning she made sandwich lunches for Natasha's father, for herself and for Natasha. They each had their own lunch box containing two rounds of sandwiches, a chunk of cheese and an apple. This was just right for one person, but not enough for two.

Natasha asked Pod. 'Why doesn't your mother give you any lunch?'

Pod shook his head. There were some things he didn't seem to want to talk about, and his mother was one of them.

Natasha tried again. 'Does she go out to work?'

'Yes. She takes the bus from the end of the road and works in a big supermarket in the town centre.'

'Does she get lunch there?'

'Yes.'

'It's a problem,' said Natasha. 'We must give it some thought.'

Her father always said that about problems. He worked in a big firm and he had to solve lots of problems. He said Natasha was going to be just like him, when she'd overcome her 'regrettable tendency to act first and think afterwards'.

Natasha said, 'The thing is, I don't mind giving you half my food, but then I'm still hungry at the end of it, and so are you. I'll ask my mummy to give me more food tomorrow.'

So Natasha did. But her mummy was in a

hurry, and said, 'Natasha, that's nonsense. You already have more to eat at lunch time than your friends do.'

'But I'm a growing girl, and besides. . . .'

'I'm late, dear, and I haven't time to argue. Give me a kiss and be off with you.'

Natasha had an idea. Sometimes her ideas were good and sometimes they weren't so good, but she felt that this one would solve everything.

'Mummy, Jesus did say we must feed the hungry, so could I bring someone back for tea today?'

'Yes, of course, dear. I'm delighted to have any of your friends to tea, you know that.'

But Natasha's mummy wasn't so delighted when she saw how much food Pod ate. Natasha's mummy was a good cook, and once a week she baked a large cake, a batch of scones and some biscuits. She put some away in the freezer, and some in the cake tin, and that would have to do till the following week when she had another baking session. But Pod ate so much that he ate up all today's cake and scones and biscuits, and tomorrow's, and the next day's.

Even Natasha was surprised at how much Pod could eat, when he put his mind to it. She wasn't doing so badly herself, because she was always hungry nowadays, having given away half her lunch.

Natasha's mummy's eyes grew bigger and bigger. She almost said 'No' when Pod asked if he could have the last biscuit.

'My!' she said, as she drained the teapot into Pod's mug. 'I'd forgotten that small boys have hollow legs!'

Pod hadn't heard this saying before, and he was so alarmed to think he had hollows in his legs that he got down from the table to inspect them. Natasha and her mummy laughed, and explained the joke to him. Pod smiled. He didn't often smile and it made Natasha feel happy to see Pod smile. He had a lovely smile which made him look like a normal boy for a change. Usually he looked pale and tired.

When Pod had gone home, Natasha tackled her mother about giving her more food in the lunch box. Natasha's mother couldn't see the point of it, so Natasha had to explain that she'd been sharing her food with Pod for a week.

'I see,' said Natasha's mummy. 'Well, your idea for solving the problem was quite good, Natasha, but I think I know a better one. I'll go to see Mrs. Pod and find out why she's not

giving Pod either food or dinner money. If she's not English, maybe she doesn't know our ways.'

So that evening when Natasha's daddy had come home from work and they'd had their supper, Natasha's mummy went to call on Mrs. Pod. She didn't come back till after Natasha had been tucked up in bed. Natasha called out that she was still awake, so her mummy came in and sat on her bed.

'What is it?' said Natasha, for her mummy looked sad.

'Oh, dear, that poor woman. She's so lonely. Her family's dead and she's lived in so many places she hasn't made any friends. Her husband is a deep sea diver, and he keeps moving around from job to job. When he brought them to England he said they'd have a permanent home here, but then he went up north after a job and she hasn't seen him for weeks. She's got herself a job to keep herself and the boy from starving, but she thought meals were provided free for all schoolchildren in England. She has her own meal at work so she hasn't been bothering to cook in the evenings. Pod said he didn't like to ask for more food, because he knew they didn't have much money. Your father and I will have to help Mrs. Pod find her way about, and in the meantime. . . .'

'We go on feeding Pod?'

'Jesus did say that we must feed the hungry and so we will. Mrs. Pod doesn't get back from work till late so we will have Pod to tea every day, and she will give us a little money towards the cost of it. And from now on, Pod will have his own packed lunch to take to school.'

'Oh, goody, goody.'

'You greedy thing!' said her mother, teasing her. And then, 'Natasha, remember to thank Jesus for showing us how to help other people. We may not be very well off ourselves, but I hope we will always have enough to share with others.'

The wedding

'Pod,' said Natasha, 'what country do you come from?'

'All over. My father is British born, but his father was from Poland. I haven't been there. My father met my mother in Italy where he was working, and we've lived in lots of places, mostly hot. But never for long. I hope we stay here for good, now.'

'Why isn't your father living with you now?'

Pod went red. 'He went north to find another job. He's a very clever man, a diver. They always send for him when there's trouble. He'll be back any day now, I expect. I wish he were back now. I wish I had a big family, like you.'

'You can have some of my aunts and uncles and cousins, with pleasure,' said Natasha. 'Especially cousin Emmy. I'll make you a free gift of her. My family thinks she's perfect and they are always saying, "Why can't you be more like Emmy, Natasha?"'

'What's wrong with her?'

'She *is* just perfect, that's what. She's clever and she's good at games and she's pretty and she never ever gets her clothes dirty!'

Pod understood. That was the nice thing about being friends with Pod. He had the same feelings as Natasha about food and games and not fussing about the occasional bit of dirt on your clothes.

Natasha sighed. 'My nicest aunt is getting married this Saturday and she's making me be a bridesmaid with Emmy. Emmy chose the pattern for the dress, and I'm going to look a freak. The dress is pink! Pink! And it's got frills all over it! I've got to wear a head-dress and have my hair curled, and throw rose petals out of a basket. I'm sure I'll tear the dress and lose the basket, and everybody will laugh!'

'I wish I could come to the wedding,' said Pod. 'My mother's working on Saturday and I'd like to see you all dressed up. I think you'd look nice. And there'd be lots to eat, wouldn't there?'

'Anybody can come to the church to watch. And if you stuck around afterwards I could sneak some food out of the reception for you, because it's being held in the church hall.'

'You're on!' said Pod.

From the moment she got up on Saturday, Natasha tried extra hard to keep clean and tidy. She wanted to please her Aunt Molly, and she didn't want her parents to be ashamed of her. She ripped one of the flounces on her dress, but her mummy put a safety-pin in it, and it hardly showed.

As they waited in the porch for the bride to arrive, Natasha peeped inside the church and saw that Pod was there. He gave her an enormous wink and held up both his thumbs to show that he thought she looked all right.

The wedding was lovely, and the bridegroom turned round and grinned at Natasha when she had a tickle in her throat and had to cough to get it out. Natasha and Emmy threw rose petals as the newly married couple came out of the church, and then they had to line up to have photographs taken. Everyone had cameras and wanted to take photographs and it was all very boring. Natasha began to fidget, especially when she saw Pod slip past the guests into the hall.

What was he up to?

When the wedding party finally got into the hall, Natasha went looking for Pod. There was the most fantastic glorious feast laid out on long tables with big white cloths on them.

Natasha knew Pod must be hiding somewhere, but she couldn't see him.

There were lots of people there, all talking and laughing, but no Pod.

'Here!' A hand reached out from under one of the long tablecloths that came down to the ground, all around a big table. Pod had hidden himself there, out of sight.

Natasha looked around, but no one was watching. She picked up a plateful of cakes and some sausage rolls, and dived under the tablecloth to be with Pod.

Pod had got some chicken drumsticks and some sandwiches, so they settled down for a quiet, enjoyable feast of their own.

'Natasha! Where is that child?' Grown-ups were calling her name.

'Take no notice,' whispered Natasha to Pod. 'They don't really want me, and anyway I can't go out now because I've got chocolate all over the front of my dress!'

'Nat . . ash . . . a! Where are you?'

'I can see her dress sticking out!' screamed cousin Emmy. 'She's under the table!'

A grown-up lifted the tablecloth to reveal two sticky children clutching empty plates.

'Natasha!' said her father, looking upset. 'How could you! And Pod!'

'It was my fault,' said Pod. 'Not hers. I was so hungry!'

'It was my fault,' said Natasha. 'I invited him to the church, and he's always hungry, so I wanted to give him some food. . . .'

Natasha's mummy looked as if she were going to cry, but Aunt Molly started to laugh. And so did her new husband. And then everyone was laughing.

'Everyone should enjoy themselves at weddings,' said Aunt Molly. 'When Jesus went to a wedding with his mother, they hadn't enough wine for all the guests to drink. Jesus didn't want anything to spoil the happiness of the day for his friends, so he worked a miracle for them. Natasha, if you had told me you wanted to invite your friend to the wedding, I'd have sent him an invitation.'

'Oh dear,' said Natasha, 'I've done it all wrong again!'

'Your heart's in the right place,' said Aunt Molly. 'Now go and wash your hands and face – and Pod, too – and we'll cut the cake.'

Pod put his right hand over his heart and made her a beautiful deep bow. 'I wish you a long life and a happy one,' he said.

'Thank you, Pod,' said Aunt Molly. 'And the same to you.'

The Good Samaritans

'Pod,' said Natasha, 'come and play.'

Pod shook his head. He was standing at the top of the road, looking up into a tree.

'Let's go to the park,' said Natasha. 'I've got some biscuits and two apples and my pocket money so's we can buy some bubblegum.'

Pod pointed upwards. 'There's a kitten up the tree and it's stuck. I don't want to leave it.'

'Cats come down by themselves. Everybody knows that.'

'This cat can't. It's too little.'

Natasha sat on the garden wall of the house nearby, and waited for Pod to get bored with the kitten, but he didn't take his eyes off it. Natasha began to get worried about the kitten, too. It was very small and it made tiny mewing sounds of distress.

'What's up?' said a neighbour on her way to the shops. Natasha explained.

'Don't worry,' said the neighbour. 'The kitten will come down when it's hungry.'

'I don't think it knows how,' said Pod.

'Tell you what,' said Natasha. 'Let's pray that Jesus will look after the kitten and make him brave enough to come down. Then we can go off to the park. It's a waste of a Saturday morning, standing here.'

'All right,' said Pod.

'Dear Jesus, please look after the kitten and get it down from the tree so that we can go off to play, Amen.'

'Amen,' said Pod, and looked up at the tree, expecting the kitten to come running down the tree trunk. But it didn't.

Natasha ran to the end of the road and back, for something to do, but Pod didn't move. Natasha gave Pod half her biscuits and one of the apples, but still the kitten didn't move.

Natasha's mummy called out that it was time for lunch. Natasha's daddy had had to go in to work on a special job that day, but Pod joined them for the meal. Unfortunately neither Natasha nor Pod could enjoy their fish fingers and ice-cream for thinking about the kitten and how hungry it must be.

'The kitten must belong to someone in one of the houses at the top of the road,' said

Natasha's mummy. 'When they find out that their kitten is in trouble, they'll fetch a ladder and get it down.'

'It's a tall tree and the kitten's a long way up,' said Natasha. 'Perhaps they haven't got a long enough ladder.'

'Then they'll call the Fire Brigade,' said Natasha's mummy. 'The Fire Brigade will bring a long ladder and get the kitten down.'

After they'd helped wash up, Natasha's mummy started to do some gardening jobs and Natasha and Pod went to see if the kitten had come down yet. It hadn't. It had stopped mewing, and was shivering.

Natasha got cross with Jesus. Hadn't they prayed for the kitten? Surely Jesus had heard them.

Then Natasha remembered about the Good Samaritan.

'Pod,' she said, 'do you remember about the Good Samaritan? He came across a man who'd been mugged and left at the side of the road to die. Lots of important people passed by, and pretended not to see the wounded man, but the Good Samaritan picked him up and took care of him. I think that the kitten is like the wounded man, and I think Jesus means us to be Good Samaritans.'

'But what can we do to help?' said Pod.

'I have an idea,' said Natasha. She held his hand because it was a scary grown-up thing they were going to do. They went to the top of the road and knocked on the door of the first house. No one in that house knew anything about the kitten, so they went on down the street, asking. At some houses they got no answer because the people were out at work.

Then a lady said, 'That kitten's a stray. The family next door have been looking after it, but when they went away on holiday, they turned the kitten out of doors to fend for itself. I'm afraid you won't find anyone to do anything about it.'

Pod tugged on Natasha's hand. 'If no one else wants it, do you think I could have it for my own? My mummy wouldn't mind. We had a cat once, but we had to leave it behind when we moved, and she cried. I didn't cry, but I did miss my cat.'

'First we have to get it down,' said Natasha. She led the way to the public telephone kiosk at the end of the road.

She said to Pod, 'You'd better do the talking, because you sound so grown up. I'll hump over, and you can climb on my back to reach the phone.'

27

Pod propped himself on Natasha's back, dialled 999 and asked for the Fire Brigade. He had such a deep voice and such a slow way of speaking that the operator thought he was a grown-up. Pod told them where he lived, and rang off.

In a few minutes a red fire engine drew up and the fireman asked, 'Where's the fire?'

Pod pointed up the tree, and the men all laughed. Natasha explained that the kitten had no one to look after it, and that it had been up there all morning and was shivering. The men stopped laughing, and put their ladder up. A large fireman went up the ladder, hooked his leg over a branch and got a grip on the kitten. By this time a lot of people had gathered around to watch, and everyone cheered when the fireman brought the kitten safely down to earth.

Pod took the kitten in his arms and stroked it until it felt better and began to purr. Natasha and Pod thanked the firemen nicely for their trouble, and then they took the kitten up to the flat in which Pod lived with his mother. They gave the kitten some milk to drink and then it washed itself all over, and went to sleep on Pod's bed.

'We'll have to give him a name,' said

Natasha. 'We'll call him Jericho because it was on the road to Jericho that the Good Samaritan saved the life of the wounded man.'

Bubblegum trouble

'Pod,' said Natasha, 'you love Jesus, so why don't you come to church on Sundays?'

'I used to go with my father,' said Pod, and looked sad. He hadn't seen his father for a long time.

'Well, why doesn't your mother bring you?'

'She says she was brought up in a different kind of church, and also she likes to lie in on Sundays.'

'We pass your flat on our way to church on Sundays. Would you like to come with us?'

'All right,' said Pod. 'But what do I have to do in your church?'

'Well, I'm in the choir and us children have to sing a special hymn for young people at the beginning of the service. . . .'

'I can't sing, you know that,' said Pod. 'The music teacher at school told me to stop singing, because I growl like a bear.'

'You can just pretend to sing, can't you? You can open and shut your mouth, and I'll sing twice as loudly and no one will notice. We only have to be in the big church for a little while, and then we go out into the hall to put our money in the collection bag. And then we go up the stairs to our own room for our own class.'

'Like any old school?'

'Not like any old school. We play games and sing rounds and do action songs and make up plays about things that happened in the Bible. And we draw and cut out, and make things. And listen to stories. It's great!'

'All right,' said Pod. 'I'll come if I can be in the choir with you, but I don't want to be left with the grown-ups. Promise?'

'Promise.'

On Sundays Natasha wore a pretty dress, of red tartan. She had a zippered pocket belt for her collection money, and her father helped her polish her sandals till they shone. She always thought she looked nice till she saw cousin Emmy join them for church. Emmy had dozens of dresses, most of them with frills on. It was most unfortunate that Natasha was in the same class as Emmy in Sunday School. Emmy was a year older than Natasha, but in the Sunday

School they had several years in one class.

Natasha could see that Pod liked their church. He sat beside her in choir and no one would have guessed he wasn't singing, he acted his part so well. Then they went out into the hall to give in their collection money. Pod was happily chewing away on his bubblegum when the bag came round to him. Natasha dropped her money into the bag and passed it to Pod. Suddenly Pod looked unhappy. Then he smiled, dropped something into the bag and passed it to Emmy on his other side.

Now Natasha had sharp eyes, and she'd seen what it was that Pod had dropped into the bag. It was his packet of bubblegum!

Natasha felt sick. When the head teacher counted the money at the end of the morning she'd find the gum and then she'd ask questions and would discover it was Pod who had put it into the bag. And then Pod would be turned out of Sunday School!

It didn't bear thinking about! Somehow Natasha had to stop it. She must get the bubblegum out of the bag before anyone counted the money.

Usually Natasha enjoyed Sunday School. Today they were acting out the story of Joseph and his marvellous coat. The teacher asked

Emmy to act the part of Joseph, and Natasha felt she could understand exactly why Joseph's brothers wanted to teach him a lesson. Natasha and Pod were acting the parts of two of the brothers, but Natasha couldn't keep her mind on what she was supposed to be doing.

Pod was all right. He seemed to be enjoying himself.

'Please miss, may I go to the toilet?' said Natasha.

'Of course,' said the teacher, 'but don't be long, love, because I want to teach you all a new action song in a minute.'

Natasha ran down the stairs and into the hall where the collection bag had been placed on top of the piano. The hall was empty. Now was her chance! She reached up on tiptoe to get the bag and at that very moment a hand was placed on her shoulder, and a voice said, 'Natasha!'

She was so startled that she grabbed the bag and pulled it towards her. The money fell out, bouncing and trickling all over the floor . . . and so did the packet of bubblegum.

'Is that what you were after?' said the head teacher, pointing to the gum.

Natasha nodded.

The teacher sat down, and pulled Natasha

onto her knee. She said, 'It wasn't your gum, was it? Did your friend Pod come without any money?'

'Don't turn him out, will you?' said Natasha. 'He does love Jesus and he won't come to church unless we bring him.'

The door opened and Pod walked in.

He said, 'Emmy saw what I did and said she'd tell on me, so I asked to go to the toilet and came down to get the gum back. My mummy did give some money for the collection, but I was hungry so I bought the gum instead. Then I thought other people might be even hungrier than me, so I put the gum into the bag.'

'I see,' said the head teacher. She put her free arm around Pod and thought about it.

Then she said, 'Do you know the story of the widow's penny? There was a rich man who put a lot of money into the collection box and boasted about it. Then along came a poor woman, who had only one penny left in all the world, but she put that in. Which one do you think Jesus loved best?'

'The poor woman,' said Natasha.

'Yes, she gave everything she had, and so did Pod. Now I don't want you to make a habit of it, Pod, because it's a lot easier for me to put money to work for Jesus, than to find a good home for some bubblegum. But this time I think I can do it. Thank you for your gift, Pod. Now run off back to your classes, both of you, and remember ... we do have a packet of biscuits and some orange squash for hungry people at the end of the morning!'

The Stilt Man

'I think he must be dead,' said Pod. He sat with his arms hunched around his legs.

Natasha knew that Pod's father had been away for a long time, and that Pod missed his father a lot.

'He doesn't have to be dead,' said Natasha. 'He's probably just bad at writing letters. Cheer up. Remember, Mummy's taking us to the Festival this afternoon.'

Pod looked brighter. 'That's good.'

'It's not all good,' said Natasha. 'Cousin Emmy's coming, too.'

Cousin Emmy had a new pink dress with a frilly petticoat to wear to the Festival, and white sandals. Natasha and Pod wore T-shirts, shorts and trainers, none of which were new. Natasha's mummy told Emmy how nice she looked, and Emmy smiled in a way which made Natasha want to slap her.

The Festival was being held in the biggest park in town. There was a giant inflatable castle and a Punch and Judy show, and a band of real live musicians. Natasha loved music which went oompa, oompa. She stood and watched the band and thought that when she grew up maybe she'd be a musician, instead of a problem-solver like her father.

'Come along, Natasha,' said her mummy. 'The others want to see the Punch and Judy.'

Natasha sighed and went along. It was remarkable, she thought, how often she had to be unselfish and do what other people wanted, instead of what she liked. She thought she'd have made a good martyr.

Natasha hadn't particularly wanted to see the Punch and Judy show, but it turned out to be a good one, which was her reward for being a martyr. The crocodile was ace, really fierce, and when the Hangman came on, she held onto Pod's hand tightly, in case he was frightened.

Emmy screamed at the Hangman, and hid behind Natasha's mummy. She would! thought Natasha.

Natasha's mummy said, 'I'm going to take Emmy off to buy some ice-creams. You two stay right there, and don't move.'

When the show had finished, Natasha said

to Pod, 'It was a bit scary though, wasn't it?'

'I wasn't looking much,' said Pod. He pointed over the heads of the crowd. 'Do you see the Stilt Man? He looks just like my dad. I thought it was him at first, but then I saw it wasn't.'

Natasha squinted against the sun and saw a tall man in a striped coat and giant-long spider-leg trousers. He had a top hat on, in the same bright colours, and he had a nice crinkly face which smiled a lot. He had fair hair and a curly beard and blue eyes and he was walking around, talking to the children. Now and then he bent down to shake hands with them.

'Let's go closer,' said Pod, and before Natasha could remind him that they were supposed to stay put, he'd wriggled off into the crowd. Natasha dived in after him, only to be caught by her mother and hauled back.

'Where do you think you're going? Where's Pod? Here, take your ice-cream before it melts.'

Emmy had a most superior smile on her face. 'I shook hands with the Stilt Man, and he admired my new dress.'

This was too much for Natasha, who pulled away from her mother's hand and went after Pod. By the time she got through the crowd, the Stilt Man was nowhere to be seen. Pod was there, looking unhappy.

He said, 'He wouldn't shake hands with me. He shook hands with all the other children, but he wouldn't shake hands with me.'

'Where is he?'

Pod pointed to a space behind one of the big tents. Natasha said, 'Come along. Maybe he didn't see you, becuse you're so small.'

They found the Stilt Man, but he looked almost normal size, because he'd lowered himself onto a stack of chairs and was reading a newspaper.

'Hello,' he said to Natasha. 'I'm having a few minutes off.'

Natasha glared up at him. 'Why didn't you shake hands with my friend Pod?'

The Stilt Man looked at Natasha and then he looked at Pod. Being a nice man, he didn't tell them to go away, even though it was his break-time.

He said, 'I'll let you into a secret. I usually work in an office, and I've only just learned how to walk on stilts, for charity. I'm a bit scared of falling, if I bend too far down. That's why I only shake hands with the bigger children. Your friend is so small, it would take a miracle for me to get down to him.'

'Do you believe in Jesus?' said Natasha.

'Well, yes, I suppose I do.'

'Then you can put your trust in him, can't you? It's very important, because you look like Pod's daddy who's gone away.'

'I see,' said the Stilt Man. 'Well, in that case, if we both pray very hard, perhaps we can manage it.' He got up, balancing himself with the aid of a tall stick. When he was standing upright, he was so tall that Pod and Natasha had to put their heads right back to look up at him.

'Oh dear,' said the Stilt Man, looking down at Pod, 'you are a long way down, aren't you? Suppose I fell on top of you?'

'You won't,' said Natasha, confidently.

The Stilt Man pulled a comical face and said, 'All right, here goes then!' He bent forward, carefully, slowly, till he was almost bent double. Until he was low enough to take Pod by the hand.

'How do you do, Pod?'

'I'm very well, thank you,' said Pod. And he smiled the biggest smile you ever did see.

'Natasha! Pod! So there you are!' Natasha's mummy came round the corner, dragging Emmy with her.

'Don't scold them, please,' said the Stilt Man, taking off his hat to Natasha's mummy. 'We

took time out to work a small miracle together, but you can have them back now. Goodbye children. Have a good time at the Festival.'

Natasha's mummy said she'd forgive them if they promised not to run off again. Then they went to have a bounce in the inflatable castle and Emmy broke the buckle of her new sandals.

It was altogether a most satisfactory day out.

The medal

'It was my birthday yesterday,' said Pod.

'Why didn't you tell me?' said Natasha. 'I would have got you a present. Are you having a party? Can I come? What sort of cake will you have?'

'My mother says she'll buy me a present next week and she did say she'd make me a special Polish cake in layers with different fillings. My father used to love that cake. But she had to work yesterday, so she couldn't.'

Pod sounded choky, and Natasha wasn't surprised. When she had a birthday she went around telling everyone beforehand, so they wouldn't forget, but Pod hadn't told anyone, not even her.

Pod said, 'I expect my dad'll send me a present next week instead.'

They were waiting at the church gates to go off for the Sunday School outing. Nearly all the parents were coming, and all the small brothers and sisters and some of the grannies and grandpas, too. They had enough cars to give lifts to everyone who hadn't a car. Pod was coming with Natasha, and they had brought enough food to include him. But at the last minute cousin Emmy decided to join them, and that was not so good.

Pod and Natasha were dressed as usual in T-shirts, shorts and trainers, but Emmy had a brand new velvety pink track suit on, and she was carrying her lunch in a matching pink case.

They went in cars to a very large park and had their lunch sitting on the grass beside a lake.

Emmy said, 'I'm good at sports. I expect I'll win most of the races and get a medal.' And she went off to practise cartwheels.

Natasha said, 'I wish she'd stayed at home.'

'Now, Natasha,' said her mother, 'that's not a very Christian attitude.'

'Well,' said Natasha, 'I wish she didn't boast so much, then.'

'That's better,' said her father, and he smiled. Natasha had a suspicion that her father didn't care much for Emmy, either. That cheered Natasha up no end.

She said, 'I wish I could win one of the

medals, and then I could give it to Pod for a present. I'm not bad at games, but Pod and I are the youngest in our Sunday School class and I don't think we stand a chance.'

'You don't have to be first *every* time,' said Natasha's father. 'The teachers are giving cards to the first three people across the line in every race. You take the cards to the scorer and he adds them up on a chart. If you can get several seconds and perhaps just one first, you might collect enough points to win a medal.'

Natasha sent up a little prayer to Jesus to let her win something, not for herself, but for Pod. She hadn't any pocket money saved to buy anything for him, and anyway, it would be much nicer to earn his present.

The first race was a sprint, and one of the big boys won that easily, with Emmy as second. Natasha just managed to scrape equal third with another boy. Pod came last.

The next race was a bean bag race and Natasha concentrated so hard that she almost came first, because most of the boys dropped their bags. But Emmy pushed Natasha aside at the last minute, so Natasha only came second.

'I told you I was good at games,' said Emmy.

Natasha nearly slapped her, but at that very moment Emmy gave a cry and clutched at her hand. She'd been stung by a bee, and although there wasn't any swelling she made such a fuss that Natasha's mummy had to bathe her hand and make her sit down to rest in the shade. And that put Emmy out of the running for the rest of the afternoon.

Natasha got a second in the sack race, and a third in the relay. Her father went over to help with the scoring, because he was so anxious to know how Natasha was doing. Pod was usually last in every race, because he was so much smaller than everyone else. He didn't seem to mind, but Natasha was upset. Why hadn't Jesus made Pod tall and strong like the other boys in the class?

Between times, her class had to wait while the Infants and the older groups of children ran their races. It was very exciting, guessing who would win.

Natasha's father said, 'Natasha, this is the last race, and if you can get a place in this, you might get a medal. But, darling, don't do yourself an injury. I'll give you some money to get Pod a present tomorrow.'

'It wouldn't be the same,' said Natasha, and she spat on her hands as she'd seen athletes do on the telly.

The last race was an obstacle race. The

whistle went and they set off towards the row of bean bags. The two biggest boys got there first. They put the bags on their heads and without dropping them had to run to the row of hoops. Natasha picked up a blue hoop and dropped it over her head. She shook it down in one swift movement, but the boys' bulkier shoulders made it more difficult for them to get through. That meant she was second as they picked up the eggs and spoons. Natasha's hand was trembling, and she put her tongue out as far as it would go, to help her balance the egg on the spoon.

But still one of the big boys was ahead of her to the sacks.

Into the sacks they went. Jump, jump, jump. The big boy was getting away from her, and then he fell down with a thump on the grass. Natasha flashed past him, hair flying all over the place. She reached the finishing line and fell over it, ahead of all the others.

She had won a first place!

She took her card and looked round to see who was going to be second, and much to her delight there was Pod, hidden almost to his shoulders in the sack, coming in behind her. Everyone else had fallen in a big heap, and they were only now picking themselves up.

'Oh, well done, Natasha!' said her father. 'And that was marvellous, Pod!'

'Do you know,' said Pod, 'this is the first time in my life that I've ever won anything?'

When they gave out the medals at the end of the afternoon, Natasha collected a beautiful big bronze medal, hanging on a red and brown striped ribbon. It was a lovely medal and it cost Natasha something to give it to Pod, but she did.

'It's yours, Pod,' she said. 'Happy Birthday.'

The accident

It was the dog's fault.

Usually Natasha crossed over the road half way along to avoid the dog, but that day they were in a hurry, and the dog didn't seem to be around, so she risked it.

It wasn't a particularly busy road, but cars did sometimes whizz through on their way to the shops. As Natasha and Pod ran past the house where the big dog lived, a milk float came along, and the dog rushed out to bark at it.

Natasha screamed and swerved into the road to avoid the dog, and at that very moment a large blue car came zooming round the corner. Natasha saw the car coming but wasn't able to stop. The milkman saw the car and shouted a warning.

Pod threw himself onto Natasha and pushed

her onto the opposite pavement, out of harm's way.

There was a bump, and after that a nasty silence, except for the dog which went on barking.

Natasha picked herself up, but Pod lay still with his eyes closed.

'They ran right across me,' said the driver, who was badly shaken. 'I couldn't help hitting the boy!'

'You were going too fast!' said the milkman.

'It was the dog,' said Natasha, and started to cry.

Someone rang for an ambulance and they lifted Pod onto a stretcher and took him away. A neighbour fetched Natasha's mummy from work, and Natasha was given a cup of sweet tea to drink and put to bed with a hot water bottle. Her mother rang the hospital and they said Pod had hurt his head and his arms and legs, but there was nothing that wouldn't mend in a few days. Only, they wanted to keep him in hospital to make sure.

'He saved my life,' said Natasha to her daddy that evening. Natasha had a lot of bumps and bruises, and was inclined to be weepy, but was otherwise all right.

'Greater love hath no man than this,' quoted

Natasha's daddy, 'that he lay down his life for his friends.'

'Pod's not going to die though, is he?'

'No, poppet, of course not. I was thinking of Jesus, who laid down his life for us. I bet he was proud of Pod this afternoon, wasn't he?'

'You can't compare Pod with Jesus. Pod's always so hungry!'

Natasha and her father both saw the funny side of that, but it didn't stop them from being worried about Pod. And they were right to be worried, because Pod didn't mend as quickly as he ought to have done. When Natasha went to see him in hospital, he didn't seem to be in any hurry to get out of bed, or even to eat anything.

'It's the shock,' the hospital said.

'It's because he's missing his father,' said Natasha to her mummy. 'How can he get better when he's not heard from his father for ages?'

'You don't understand, poppet.'

'I do understand,' said Natasha, crossly. 'Some grown ups quarrel and decide to live apart and then there's a divorce and the children get the worst of it as usual.'

'Natasha!'

'Well, I think someone ought to write to Pod's father and tell him how much Pod is missing him, and then he would come to see Pod straight away.'

'Mrs. Pod has done that, poppet,' said Natasha's mummy. 'And he's written back to say that he's too busy. It's very sad, and I don't know what we can do about it, except pray.'

'I pray for Pod every night and every morning, and every time in between when I think about him.'

The days came and went and Pod didn't seem to get any better. The Sunday School teachers often gave Mrs. Pod a lift to the hospital, and so did Natasha's father and mother.

One evening, after seeing Pod, Natasha went to sit on her father's knee. He held her tightly.

'Cheer up, sweetheart. Remember, it's your birthday next week.'

'I can't think about birthdays when Pod is so poorly. He's not getting any better, is he? Why doesn't Jesus make him well again?'

'When I was praying for Pod last night,' said her father, 'he put it into my head that there was something I could do, to show Pod that we all love him. I'm going to write to the newspapers, to tell them how Pod saved your life. Perhaps that might make him feel better, and want to get well again.'

So next week there was an article in the local

paper about Pod, with a photograph, and on Sunday afternoon while Natasha was sitting with Pod, there was a disturbance just inside the door of the ward, with the nurses all laughing. Then the oddest-looking man came into view, unfolding himself till he was so tall that they had to hold their heads back to look up at him.

'Look, Pod!' cried Natasha. 'It's the Stilt Man!'

The Stilt Man walked down the ward, with the children on either side laughing and clapping, till he came to Pod's bed.

He took off his hat, and bowed low to Pod. He said, 'Young man, I recognised your photo in the papers. That was a brave thing you did, and I hope they give you a medal for it. But in the meantime, I'd be delighted to shake your hand.'

He leaned right over and took Pod's hand in his, and shook it. He went round the ward and shook hands with all the other children, too. Then he sat down beside Pod and talked to him for a long time about his friends and his cat, and his school, and his church and everything. He laughed so much when Pod told him about putting the bubblegum in the collection, that Natasha said, 'Well, why don't you come to our church, too?'

'I just might at that,' said the Stilt Man. 'I'm not going to lose touch with you two in a hurry. Now, Pod, promise me you'll get better now?'

'Oh, yes,' said Pod, who was actually sitting straight up in bed for a change. 'I think I feel hungry already!'

A week later he came to Natasha's birthday party. He was still looking pale and weak, but he ate everything in sight, and he beat Emmy in the treasure hunt. All the people Natasha liked best in the world came, including her favourite Aunt Molly and her new husband, the Stilt Man, and, of course, Mrs. Pod. Natasha had lots of presents, but the one she liked best of all came from Pod. His daddy had sent him some money for a Get Well present, and Pod had bought Natasha her very own fish badge to wear, so that everyone could see she loved Jesus.

NATASHA'S SWING

Contents

The swing

Cousin Emmy had lots of expensive playthings in her garden, but somehow it was never convenient for Pod and Natasha to play there. They didn't mind, because they found plenty to do in Natasha's garden. They climbed the laburnum tree and pretended that they were pirates, or they played shipwreck, jumping from one old garden sack to another without landing on the grass. Or French cricket. They never seemed to run out of ideas of things to do.

But as often as not, Cousin Emmy would come wandering in and bother them, wanting to play dolls' tea parties and baby games like that.

One day Natasha's father took a long piece of rope and cut it into four. He drilled holes near the four corners of a thick piece of wood. The ropes went through the holes and were knotted on the underside. Then Natasha's father tied the top ends of the ropes to the stout branch of the big tree at the bottom of their garden . . . and they had their very own swing!

'Super fantastic!' said Natasha, grabbing the swing. 'Thanks a trillion, Dad.' Then she saw Pod's face, and said, 'No, you go first, and I'll push you really high.'

Pod's face took on the look he wore when eating chocolate. He'd never had a proper go on a swing before, except sometimes in the park. This was miles better. Even Natasha, who desperately wanted a go, was happy, pushing Pod higher and higher till his toes almost touched the leaves of the tree.

'Now me,' said Natasha. Pod nodded and got off the swing.

'I don't think much of your swing,' said someone. Natasha and Pod stopped smiling. They knew the voice of Cousin Emmy only too well.

Cousin Emmy was wearing another new dress, and she had a glittery bow on her hair. She said, 'My father bought me a proper swing on a metal frame, and of course I've got bars for practising my athletics, as well. Is this the best your father can do?'

Natasha thought, Oh doom and gloom! She'd heard her father say that once, and she'd remembered it, because it was the sort of saying that might come in useful one day. She exchanged looks with Pod. Perhaps if they ignored Cousin Emmy, she might go away. Natasha seated herself on the swing, but Emmy laid hold of one of the ropes, and wouldn't let go.

Natasha's mummy must have been watching from the house, because now she called out, 'Natasha, let Emmy have a go!'

Natasha got off the swing, feeling that life was very unfair. Hadn't she been even better than good, letting Pod have first go?

Emmy got onto the swing, settled her skirts, and began to push. She didn't get very high.

'Go on!' she said. 'Push me! I want to go really high!'

Natasha ground her teeth, but she pushed. And pushed. And pushed. She pushed till she felt dizzy, and then she stopped.

'Go on!' shrieked Emmy. 'What are you stopping for!'

'I'm tired,' said Natasha. 'And anyway, it's my turn.'

'No, it isn't. I haven't finished yet.'

'Yes, you have. It's my swing, and you've had ever such a long turn, and I haven't had a go yet.'

By now the swing had almost stopped. Natasha pulled at the rope, but Emmy stuck to the seat, and even slapped Natasha's hand away.

'What are you doing?' called out Natasha's mummy.

'It's my turn!' yelled Natasha, who was beginning to lose her temper.

'I've only just got on!' whined Emmy.

Natasha's mummy said, 'Well, let her have a proper go, Natasha.'

Cousin Emmy smiled. 'Go on, push me. You've

got to!'

'I won't!' said Natasha, going red. 'Get . . . off my . . . swing!'

'Shan't!'

Natasha didn't stop to count ten. She picked up her cricket bat and whacked Cousin Emmy. Cousin Emmy screamed and Natasha's mummy shot out of the house, dishcloth in hand.

'She hit me!' screeched Emmy.

'Natasha! Go up to your room at once!' Natasha's mummy gave her such a smack that she almost cried, too. She stomped off up the garden, slammed the door and went up to her room.

After a while there was a thud on the window pane, where someone had thrown a lump of earth at it. Natasha opened the window, because she knew Pod would go on throwing things till she did.

He was looking miserable. 'I told your mummy that Emmy wouldn't get off the swing, but she wouldn't listen. Emmy's making out she's really badly hurt!'

'I wish she were,' said Natasha.

'If only you hadn't hit her, we could have worked it out.'

'Mummy always takes her side! It's not fair!'

They talked about it for a bit, and then Pod had to go home. After a while Natasha's mummy came up.

'Well, Natasha, are you ready to apologise to Emmy?'

'I don't see why I should, when it was all her

fault. Why does she have to come here and spoil everything?'

'Because she's got no one else to play with. Natasha, try to understand. Emmy's parents have lots of money, but they work so hard they are hardly ever at home. Emmy needs friends. I know she can be a little difficult, but that's mostly because she doesn't get enough love at home. Now, you know what Jesus said about loving your neighbour. . . '

'Neighbours don't cheat,' said Natasha. 'Emmy's a cheat and a tell-tale and I hate her!'

'Jesus loved even those who killed him. Let's think about that, shall we? And then we will pray about it. Pray that he will help you to love her.'

'All right,' said Natasha. 'I'll ask Jesus to help, but I can't guarantee miracles!' And then both Natasha and her mummy got the giggles, because if there was one person who was rather good at miracles, it was Jesus. And somehow, after she'd prayed a bit, Natasha did begin to feel calmer, and even to feel sorry – just a little bit – that she'd hit Emmy.

When she went downstairs with her mummy, Emmy was sitting in Natasha's chair, eating chocolate biscuits and drinking coke. She looked so uppity that Natasha almost growled at her instead of saying she was sorry, but somehow she got the words out. She felt better, straight away.

'That's all right,' said Emmy. 'Your mummy says I can have as many goes on the swing as I want, and that you've got to push me!'

'But only,' said Natasha's mummy, 'if you take it strictly in turn. It's Natasha's swing, and she hasn't had a go yet. Emmy, you must push Natasha first, and then you can have a turn later. And I'll be watching to see fair play.'

Bad dreams

Pod was so excited he couldn't keep still. He stood on one leg, to stop himself jumping around. Then he hopped up and down on the same spot. His mother was going up north to visit his father. Pod couldn't go because the train fare was so expensive, so he was going to spend the weekend with Natasha instead.

After school on Friday, Pod carried Jericho the kitten in his school satchel, and Natasha helped him along with his bag. The tins of cat food and his computer game were on top, being the most important, but he forgot to pack his pyjama top. Natasha's mummy said he could wear an old T-shirt of Natasha's in bed, so that was all right.

Jericho was excited, too. Jericho didn't have much sense, for a cat. Some cats have a lot of sense, and know when not to get under people's feet, but Jericho was stupid that way. He nearly tripped Natasha's mummy up, just as she was carrying the casserole to the table, and he thought Natasha's daddy's screwdriver was a special toy for him to play with. He spun it round and round with his paw, till it dropped off the table and hid itself in a crack between two cupboards.

Natasha's mummy got cross, and said Jericho would have to go back to the flat and stay there all alone, if Pod couldn't control him. So Pod put Jericho back into his satchel while they had supper, and then he and Natasha took the kitten outside for a game in the garden.

They had a lovely time playing hide and seek with Jericho and then Cousin Emmy arrived to tell them about her father's new video. She said she'd been watching a real-grown up horror film, and it had given her bad dreams, thinking the werewolf was after her in the night.

'What's a werewolf?' said Pod. 'I've never heard of one. You're making it up.'

'Don't you know anything?' said Cousin Emmy, all superior. 'It's a man by day, and a wolf by night. And it bites other animals, and they become wolves at night, too, and they go around sniffing, with their tongues hanging out, and when they find a house with children in it, they break in, and. . . '

'That's enough,' said Natasha's mummy. 'You'll give Pod and Natasha bad dreams, too.'

'I had terrible bad dreams,' said Emmy, wriggling and grinning. 'I dreamed our old dog turned into a wolf last night and was trying to sniff his way up the stairs to get me. . . . '

'What nonsense, Emmy,' said Natasha's

mummy. 'That's more than enough, and anyway it's time for you to go home, and time for Natasha and Pod to go to bed, too.'

Jericho usually slept on Pod's bed, but Natasha's mummy didn't like cats going upstairs, so she said Jericho must be shut up in the dining-room for the night, where he couldn't do any damage. They had fixed him up with a box with some cat litter in it, just in case.

Natasha and Pod went quietly up the stairs, got undressed, had a good wash, cleaned their teeth and got into bed. Pod was sleeping in a camp bed in Natasha's room, to be friendly.

Natasha's mummy heard their prayers, and tucked them up for the night. Then she turned out the light, and went downstairs.

'Wrrf!' said Natasha. 'Pod, do you feel like playing at werewolves? I'll chase you, with my tongue hanging out, and then you can chase me. Bed's safe, but anywhere else, the werewolf can get me!'

'Wrrf, Wrrf!' said Pod, enthusiastically. They chased one another all over the room till Natasha fell over the camp bed and her mother came up to say they'd have to sleep in separate rooms if they couldn't be quiet and go to sleep.

So they got back into bed and thought about this and that for a while.

'There isn't really any such thing as a werewolf, is there?' said Natasha at last.

'Shouldn't think so,' said Pod. 'But I can't help

worrying about Jericho downstairs, all on his own. I don't really suppose a werewolf would come along, but. . .'

'Let's have a pray for him,' said Natasha. 'Just in case.'

'Right!' said Pod. 'Please, Jesus, keep Jericho safe. Amen!'

'And don't forget us, either,' said Natasha. 'Amen.'

They felt better after that, and soon fell asleep. Pod woke up first, in the pale light of dawn, and looked around him in a daze. He'd been having a bad dream. At first he couldn't think where he was, and then he remembered about his mother going away, and about his coming to stay with Natasha, and about Jericho and the werewolf.

Suddenly he reached over and clutched at Natasha's arm. She woke up, and he put his hand over her mouth to stop her screaming. For down below they could hear something rolling and bumping . . . and then there was a thud and another rolling sound.

'The werewolf!' squeaked Natasha, in a muffled sort of way. Pod got out of bed. He was shivering, but he had a determined look on his face.

'Don't, Pod! He'll kill you!'

'It's my kitten,' said Pod, 'and I'm not going to let any old werewolf bite my kitten and turn him into a wolf!'

'But suppose he has, already! Suppose Jericho is a wolf already, and is snuffling around, trying to

find us. . . !'

'Can't help it,' said Pod, opening the door. 'Got to find out!'

'Wait for me!' said Natasha. 'Perhaps if there's two of us, he won't know which to bite first!'

The children crept out onto the landing and listened. There was nothing to be seen on the stairs. No wolf, no nothing.

Bump . . . rrroll . . . crash!

Natasha found Pod's hand and held on tight, in case he was frightened. They inched their way down the stairs. There wasn't any wolf in the hall, either. The dining-room door was shut.

Pod took a deep breath and turned the handle. The door creaked open, and there, on the carpet just inside the door, was a bright green apple! A little further off was a large orange.

And rolling over and over towards them came another apple!

Jericho was on the dining-room table, and was hooking oranges and apples out of the fruit bowl to play with. When the apples and oranges reached the end of the table, they rolled off, and bumped and rolled all over the floor – which was what the children had heard upstairs.

'You know something?' said Natasha. 'It's a good thing we had a bit of a pray for Jericho last night. I'm sure that kept him safe. And us, too.'

The jumble sale

Natasha's mother and father were organising a jumble sale at the church. They needed lots of help, so Natasha and Pod went along to see what they could do.

Natasha said, 'Mummy's promised to get me a jigsaw puzzle and some dressing-up clothes from the jumble, if I'm good.'

'My mum wants to look out for some clothes for me,' said Pod. 'And she said if there were a toy I wanted, she'd buy it for me.'

The jumble sale was being held in the big church hall. There was a mountain of black plastic sacks to be sorted out on the stage, and when they arrived, the other helpers were just standing around, doing nothing.

'Right!' said Natasha's mummy. 'If we don't make a start we'll never finish. Children's clothing goes on the tables on the right, women's and girls' over there, and men's clothing in the middle. We'll put a table here for shoes and handbags, and all the bric-a-brac can go at the far end.'

'There's a lot of kitchen stuff,' said one of the helpers. 'Glasses, plates, knives and forks, pots and pans. . . '

'We'll put a couple of tables for them up against the stage.'

Natasha and Pod got all hot and tired, dragging things out of bags and carrying them to the right tables. It seemed that as fast as they cleared one bag, someone brought in two more.

Suddenly they heard a familiar voice. 'Of course,' said Cousin Emmy, 'we don't have to buy things in jumble sales, but I've brought some of my old toys for you to sell. Mother says it can be my good deed for the day.'

'Oh, gloom and doom!' said Natasha to Pod, but he wasn't listening, for he'd found a computer game in perfect working order, with batteries included.

'Just look at this!' he said. 'I've always wanted one, but they're far too expensive for Mum to buy. Do you think they'd let her buy it for me tomorrow?'

Cousin Emmy snatched it from him. 'Why, it's like one of mine, only better. I'll get my mother to buy it for me.'

Natasha said, 'Emmy, you greedy thing. . .'

'Now, now,' said her daddy, taking the game off Emmy and putting it on a high ledge. 'No squabbling over the spoils. Emmy, have you come to help? That's nice. Helpers get first pick of the goods.'

Emmy got the message. Sort jumble, or else! So she went to try on some shoes on a nearby table.

'Look what I've found!' said Pod. Under the now disappearing piles of black sacks were two large laundry baskets with lids. Pod stood on a battered suitcase and started throwing things out. Natasha was that little bit taller and could get the top things out by herself, but after a while they both had to tilt the baskets and then roll them over to get at the things in the bottom. When Pod got near the end of his basket, he crawled inside to get at the very last things . . . which turned out to be a couple of children's books.

'I've got a copy of this at home,' said Natasha, looking at the top book. 'Look, it's Ali Baba and the Forty Thieves, and their baskets are just like these laundry baskets.'

'I don't know that story,' said Pod.

'Well, some thieves got themselves carried into a palace in big baskets, so that when the signal was given, they could jump out of their hiding places and kill everyone. And Ali Baba learned about it, and he went round sticking his sword into all the baskets so that the robbers died, and when it was time for them to come out, they couldn't because they were deaded.'

'The baskets do look like the ones in the book,' said Pod. 'Let's play we're thieves, and jump out at one another.'

'Let's!' agreed Natasha, climbing into her basket.

'I'll be the Magnificent Moustachio, the captain of the wicked thieves!'

'And I'll be Mr Abracadabra, the baddest of the lot!'

They jumped up and down like jack-in-the-boxes, and made so much noise that the grown-ups told them to be quiet, and Cousin Emmy came up to ask what they were playing.

'Ali Baba and the Forty Thieves.'

'I'll put the lids on for you then,' said Cousin Emmy, and there was something in her voice which ought to have warned Pod and Natasha that she was up to no good.

She put on the lids, and fastened them down.

'There's plenty of room,' said Pod. 'Woowoo! I'm Mr Abracadabra, and I'm the biggest and baddest of the robbers, and I'm going to jump out and frighten you. . .'

'It's a bit squeezy,' said Natasha. 'It must have been hard for them to keep still for so long. Let us out now, Emmy.'

But Emmy didn't. 'You can jolly well stay there till I've got the computer game, so there!'

She jumped off the stage and ran away.

'Help!' cried Pod and Natasha.

But the grown-ups were having a much needed cup of tea at the far end of the hall, and no one took any notice.

Natasha started rocking her basket to and fro. Pod jumped up and down. The two baskets rocked and hopped about the stage. They lurched this way

and they lurched that way. Pod in his basket bumped against the back wall and then . . . and then he tipped over and began to roll . . . and as he rolled, so he collided with Natasha in her basket, and they both rolled down the stage . . . and fell with a thump onto the tables below which had been set out with all the kitchen things!

Crash . . . crash . . . smash!

Pots and pans went this way, a pair of saucepans that, and a whole pile of plates slithered onto the floor and shattered into hundreds of pieces!

The grown-ups screamed and shouted and got very angry, but Natasha's daddy got the children out of the baskets and took them aside to recover, and to explain.

Natasha's daddy had a job keeping his face straight when he heard what had happened, but finally he said, 'The Bible teaches us that the workman deserves his wages. Pod, you get the computer game for whatever pocket money you've got. And Natasha, I've found a smashing great big jigsaw for you that's absolutely complete.'

'Great!' said Natasha. 'Only, what about the mess we made of the kitchen jumble?'

'I think,' said Natasha's daddy, 'that Cousin Emmy should clear that up, don't you?'

And he stood over her while she did it, too!

Running away

'I'm fed up!' said Natasha to Pod as they walked home from school one Friday afternoon. 'It's worse than doom and gloom. Cousin Emmy is coming to stay for half-term. I'm thinking of running away.'

'Good idea,' said Pod. 'Let's go to Scotland to visit my dad.'

'Brill!' said Natasha, cheering up. 'We can spend half-term with him, and come back when Cousin Emmy's gone. How do we get there?'

'We'll hitch-hike,' said Pod. 'I know the way because I heard a man telling a hitch-hiker about it the other day. We go straight up the North Circular and on to the M1. We can start tomorrow morning, after breakfast. I'll ask my mum for extra food for an all-day picnic, and say I'm coming to stay the day with you.'

'And I'll do the same. We'd better leave notes on our pillows, so they won't worry.'

So next morning they set out. Natasha had her sandwiches in her lunch box and a compass that she'd got in a cracker. It was a bit difficult to see how the compass worked because it usually stuck at SW, but if she jiggled it, then it moved.

Pod had his satchel on his back, but something kept moving around, making bumps in it.

'I've brought my computer game and Jericho,' said Pod. 'I know my dad will want to see the game, and I couldn't leave Jericho alone in the flat.'

They walked up the road in the hot sun and turned left, and left again, till they reached the North Circular. It was a very busy road with lots of noisy traffic on it. It smelt of petrol. Even the leaves on the trees looked dusty, and the noise was so thunderous, you couldn't talk properly.

They came to a gigantic roundabout where the North Circular crossed another main road. You couldn't get across it at road level, but had to go down some steps into a subway. Then you came out in a sort of sunken garden place in the middle of the roundabout, and took another subway under another road and climbed some more steps up to the other side of the road.

When the children got to the middle of the roundabout they stopped. There were grassy slopes all around, planted with shrubs. It was a marvellous place for a picnic, and they felt hungry and a bit tired after walking all that way.

So they sat down under some bushes away from the path, and Pod undid the straps of his satchel, to get at his food.

That did it! Jericho sprang out and dived into

the bushes. He thought they were playing hide and seek.

'Whee-ee!' screamed Natasha. 'Let's play we're cowboys chasing a runaway steer, like in the westerns on the telly!'

'Yippee!' cried Pod and leaped at Jericho, but the kitten escaped and ran into the middle of a thorny bush. Natasha stopped being a cowboy, and tried to coax Jericho out, while Pod tried to creep up on him from behind. Just as they thought they'd got him, Jericho whisked out from under their fingers and scampered up the slope. The roundabout was huge, and Jericho thought it was even better than playing in Natasha's garden. He whisked in and out of the bushes. He crouched, rump swaying, and darted off as soon as the children got near him. Just as they thought they'd lost him for good, he ran out from under a bush and pounced on Natasha's shoe-lace, and tried to bite it off.

Natasha squealed and laughed and fell over . . . and then Pod fell over her, too. So Jericho went and hid himself in some long grass till he got hungry and came out, mewing for food. Pod had brought a small bottle of milk for Jericho and some of his special biscuits. He tied Jericho to the handle of his satchel, so that he couldn't run away again while the children ate their own food.

'That was fun!' said Natasha, flattening herself on the grass for a rest. It was very hot in the sun, and Jericho had quite worn her out.

They stopped where they were for a bit, not quite dropping off to sleep, but not inclined to move, either.

At last Pod said that perhaps they ought to be moving on, because they'd got a long way to go yet. They put Jericho back into the satchel, but couldn't decide which of the subways they ought to take to get to Scotland. Just when they needed it, Natasha's compass refused to work.

'We must ask someone who looks nice,' said Natasha. 'Someone like that old lady over there.'

'Scotland?' the old lady said, looking surprised. 'You're hitch-hiking to Scotland? That's a long way off, my dears, and it's dangerous for children to ask just anyone for a lift. Do your parents know what you're doing?'

'Yes, of course,' said Natasha. 'We left them notes, and it's quite all right because we're going to stay with Pod's father on an oil rig.'

'I don't think it's all right at all,' said the old lady. 'I think I'd better take you along to the nearest police station. . .'

'We were only joking!' said Natasha, backing away. She and Pod dived into the nearest subway and ran and ran and ran. At last they came to a seat outside some shops, and collapsed.

Natasha looked about her. 'Do you think we took the wrong turning? This doesn't look like the M1.'

Pod was counting his pocket money. 'I've got enough for an ice cream, I think.'

They shared the ice cream, taking licks in turn; one for Pod, one for Natasha and one for Jericho. Then they sat looking at the traffic, and thinking about food, and home.

Pod said, 'My mum will be back home by now, perhaps. We were going to have fish and chips for supper. Or sausages, maybe.'

'Perhaps,' said Natasha, 'we could go back home, and try again some other time. I could tell my daddy about not wanting Cousin Emmy to stay, and perhaps he could fix it so she didn't.'

'And I could ask my mum to phone my dad, and perhaps he could come and fetch us to stay with him. Which way should we go?'

Natasha sighed, the sort of sigh which started in her trainers, and finished at the ends of her hair. She said, 'I don't know, either.' If she'd been the sort of child that cried, she might have felt like it, then. She knew Pod wouldn't cry, because he never did, even when he hurt himself really badly in the playground.

She said, 'If Jesus were around, he'd come and find us. Because we're just like two of his lost sheep, aren't we?'

'I suppose it wouldn't do any harm to have a pray about it,' said Pod. 'We could ask him to send someone to find us . . . if they weren't too busy or anything.'

Natasha closed her eyes and prayed really hard. And just at that very moment a car drove up, and Natasha's daddy got out.

'Natasha! Pod!'

He picked them up and hugged them. He said he'd been looking everywhere for them, and so had Natasha's mummy, and Pod's mummy.

'Just like the good shepherd and the lost sheep in Jesus' story,' said Natasha. 'We were trying to run away, but we're quite happy to come home now.'

'Very happy,' said Pod. 'What's for supper?'

The office

Natasha's mummy had taken the three children to buy shoes. Pod and Natasha had chosen new trainers in less time than it takes to chew a couple of Smarties, but Cousin Emmy didn't want trainers, or plimsolls, or lace-ups, or buttoned shoes. She wanted a pair of fashion shoes, and she couldn't decide which colour she should have.

Natasha and Pod could see that they were going to waste the whole morning in the shoe shop, if they didn't do something about it. Just at that moment they saw a familiar figure walk by.

'Mum,' said Natasha, jumping off her seat, 'I saw the Stilt Man walk past. Can we go and say hello to him?'

'Yes, but don't leave the shopping centre, and don't be a bother to him, will you, Natasha?'

Natasha and Pod shot out of the shop, just as the Stilt Man walked through the big glass doors of the office block next door. The Stilt Man wasn't wearing his stripey clothes today, but they caught sight of his nice grey suit disappearing off the top of the escalator that took people upstairs.

Natasha jumped onto the escalator, pulling Pod on after her. He wasn't always exactly sure where to put his feet on escalators, but Natasha said you could always shift your feet, after you got on.

They called after the Stilt Man to stop, but he didn't hear them. As they got off the first escalator, he was just getting off the second, so they followed him up . . . and up . . . and up.

They stepped off on the top floor and saw a grey suit following a food trolley through a door at the end of the passage. The trolley had white cloths on it, and there were plates of sandwiches and cups and saucers and a coffee pot on it.

Pod said, 'I'll bet the Stilt Man would give me something to eat if he knew how hungry I was.' And he followed the trolley.

Natasha wavered. There were grown-ups coming and going and she wasn't exactly sure, all of a sudden, that the Stilt Man would have time to see them today. But Pod had disappeared through the door, so she followed, into a big office.

The Stilt Man wasn't there. There was a woman sitting behind a huge desk, and there was a man in a grey suit, who was holding a lot of papers, but he didn't look anything like the Stilt Man.

The woman was wearing glasses. She looked at the children and said, 'Well?' Natasha had been thinking how very interesting it was to go into a real grown-up office, so Pod replied for them both.

'Please, we were looking for our friend the Stilt Man to say hello, and I thought maybe he'd give us a biscuit, or even a sandwich, if he knew how hungry I was.'

'The Stilt Man?' repeated the woman, flashing her glasses at them. 'Who or what is a Stilt Man?'

Natasha stopped thinking that she'd like to play with all the buttons sticking out of the box on the woman's desk, and started to feel that maybe it was time that they left. But of course she must be polite about it, and explain, or maybe they'd get the Stilt Man into trouble.

'Please, the Stilt Man is a friend of ours, who dresses up and walks on stilts for charity. We saw him come up the stairs, and then we lost him.'

'Ah!' said the man with all the papers, to the woman behind the desk. 'You remember we had a lot of people applying for the job of Events Organiser? We short-listed two, and asked them to come back today, for a further interview. It must be one of them.'

'If this Stilt Man, or whatever his name is, is responsible for these children,' said the woman, 'then get him in here, straight away.'

The man got busy pressing knobs and speaking into a box, and the Stilt Man came in, looking worried.

'Hey kids,' he said. 'You shouldn't be here.' He turned to the woman behind the desk and said, 'Sorry. These are two friends of mine. I'll take them away.'

'Wait!' said the woman, and when she said 'Wait!' like that, you waited. 'I wasn't aware you did charity work in your own time.'

'It amuses the kids. They seem to like it.'

The woman took hold of the papers the man was holding, and studied them. She said, 'You will have to be good with children, for this job. Tell me a children's story. Now. Tell me the story of the Pied Piper.'

The Stilt Man looked upset. Natasha had a feeling that maybe he wasn't too well acquainted with that particular story. She was beginning to think that she and Pod had done the wrong thing, barging in like this. And if they had messed up his interview . . . well, it didn't bear thinking about! She wished she could do something to help, but she couldn't think what, so she had a little pray about it.

An idea popped into her head, and she tugged on the Stilt Man's hand, to whisper in his ear.

The Stilt Man nodded, and began to smile. He said, 'One day Jesus was busy with all his grown-up friends, and the children couldn't get anywhere near him. They tried this way and they tried that, but the grown-ups kept saying, "Go away; he's too busy to see you". But Jesus heard, and told his friends to let the children come to him. He was never too busy to see the children.'

The man with the papers said, 'That's not the Pied Piper story!'

'Yes, it is!' said Natasha indignantly. 'It's the best Pied Piper story I know, and it really wasn't

the Stilt Man's fault that we followed him.'

'Except,' said the woman, 'that he's obviously a sort of Pied Piper himself, because he made you want to be with him. We need a Pied Piper in this job. Raising money for a children's charity requires something more than just business experience. When can you start?'

The Stilt Man looked surprised. 'You mean, I get the job?'

'Provided,' said the woman, smiling rather grimly, 'that you take those children out of here before the girl has fused all the wires on my intercom, and the boy has eaten the last of my lunch!'

Natasha hastily withdrew her forefinger from the tempting buttons, and Pod made the woman a low bow, while stuffing the last of the sandwich he had taken into his mouth. She was actually laughing as they backed out of the office.

Going back down the escalators, the Stilt Man held on to the children tightly.

'She didn't really mind us barging in, did she?' said Natasha. 'I suppose we shouldn't have, really, but it was all so interesting!'

Pod sighed. 'I'm still hungry. Sandwiches don't really fill you up properly, do they?'

The Stilt Man laughed and laughed. He said, 'If you hadn't prompted me, I'd never have remembered that story about Jesus, and I don't suppose I'd have got the job!'

They got back to the shop to find Natasha's

mummy paying for the shoes. And then the Stilt Man took them all off to MacDonald's to celebrate.

The toy service

'I hate Christmas,' said Pod.

Natasha was colouring a Christmas card, with her tongue out to help her get round the twiddly bits. She said, 'I think Christmas is lovely. The best time of the year.'

Pod hadn't touched the card he was supposed to be colouring. He said, 'I'm not going to make any cards. I'm not going to make any presents. I won't be a king in the nativity play, and I'm not going to sing any carols, either. I'm going on strike till it's all over.'

Natasha sucked the end of her felt-tipped pen, the way her mother always told her not to. One of the pens had leaked and got itself onto her T-shirt. She tried to rub it off, but couldn't. She sighed. She knew she'd get into trouble about that.

She said, 'You can't go on strike. You won't get any presents if you do.'

'Shan't get any, anyway. Mum says it's too expensive for us to go up north to be with my dad, and he can't get the time off to come down here. She says it's all she can do to get me some new shoes and shirts for Christmas, and I mustn't expect anything fancy.'

'All right, but you can make her something.'

'I asked her what she wanted and she said not to bother, so I won't. She says it's all a big con trick, anyway, everyone buying things, just so's the shops can make a lot of money. Look at your cousin Emmy.'

'Yuk!' said Natasha. 'Do I have to?'

Pod almost smiled. 'Well, you see what I mean. She's had her list of things she wants for Christmas made out for ages. All she thinks about is getting lots of expensive things to play with, and she won't really like them, when she does get them.'

Natasha put her pen down and thought about Pod's problem.

'But Christmas isn't really about trees and presents and eating lots of nice things. It's about remembering how Jesus was born and how that makes everyone happy. It's because it makes us happy that we have a good time and give one another presents. That's why we give some of our good toys next Sunday, at the special toy service.'

'I'm not going,' said Pod. 'Haven't got anything to give, anyway.'

Pod meant what he was saying. That was one of the problems with Pod; when he made up his mind about something, he stuck to it.

Natasha could understand about his not wanting

to give anything at the toy service. Pod hadn't got anything much in the way of toys. His kitten was the best thing he had, and then the computer game he'd got in the jumble sale. He had a couple of jigsaws, not quite complete, and a painting set, and that was about all.

Natasha tried to think what it was like to be Pod at Christmas, without any family around him except his mother. She didn't think she'd like it much, either.

She tried to look on the bright side. 'Well, I like Christmas, anyway. I like helping Daddy decorate, and get out the crib that he made for me. I like to think about Jesus as a cuddly little baby that you could hold in your arms. And I like making things for people. We haven't got much money to spare, but it gives me a lovely feeling to give presents to people. It doesn't have to cost a lot from the shops. Think about the shepherds; they would have given what they had . . . a pipe, a lamb, a bunch of berries. I like the shepherds better than the kings, don't you? I mean, the kings weren't giving things which cost them so much, because they had plenty to start with.'

'Forget it,' said Pod.

'I'm not saying it's easy, giving things,' said Natasha, chewing her pen. 'I'm not exactly looking forward to finding something nice from my toy cupboard to give away on Sunday. I know the toys go to children who haven't got much of anything, so the toys have got to be good . . . but you know there aren't many toys in my cupboard which are absolutely perfect. And those that are good, I haven't really finished with yet.'

It hurt to think of parting with toys you were fond of, but it hurt even more to think of Pod not having anything to put under the tree on Sunday. It seemed to her that Pod ought to be receiving a good toy, not having to give one away.

She had an idea. 'How about if I find two good toys to give away? One for me, and one for you? My train set, maybe.'

Pod went red. 'But you love that, and we play with it quite often.'

'Yes, but maybe some other child needs it more than we do, and I expect some people would think it was a bit of a baby toy, anyway.'

Pod kicked the table legs. 'Well, don't bother for me. I told you, I'm not going to the toy service, anyway.'

And when Natasha and her family went to collect Pod on their way to church on Sunday, he said he wasn't coming. Natasha was clutching the train set and her best jigsaw (absolutely complete) and was all prepared to give him one to carry, but he wouldn't come.

Natasha said to her mummy, 'It's because he's going to be so lonely at Christmas. Do you think we could ask him and his mummy for Christmas Day?'

'What, in addition to your Aunt Molly and Uncle Tom, and the old woman down the road, and the man who hasn't anywhere else to go? Oh, well! I suppose we can fit them in somehow. Yes, of course I'll ask them!'

'Can I run back and tell him now?'

'No, we'll be late for church, tell him later.'

Natasha felt better about that, but worse when she got into church without Pod. And she felt even more awful when she saw the pile of expensive toys Cousin Emmy was going to put under the tree. Suddenly her own gifts seemed very shabby.

The children formed up into a line, carrying their toys, and started to walk through the church to put their presents under the tree. Natasha walked at the end by the teacher. She put her presents down, and went to join Cousin Emmy in the choir ... and then they heard someone come running down the church. Everyone looked round to see who it was.

And there was Pod, carrying his one and only, his beautiful, much loved computer game. He put it down, very carefully, under the tree and then slipped into the pew at Natasha's side.

'Sorry I'm late,' he said. He was smiling, in a shiny sort of way.

'You're to come to us for Christmas Day,' Natasha whispered as the first hymn was announced.

'Great!' said Pod. 'That'll be just great!'

Santa Claus

Sometimes it was hard for Natasha to remember that she ought to love everyone. Especially Cousin Emmy. Cousin Emmy went to church but somehow it didn't seem to make much difference to the way she behaved. Natasha knew her mummy wanted them to be special friends, but it wasn't easy.

Cousin Emmy took the last biscuit, without asking if either Natasha or Pod wanted it. She said, 'I'm really looking forward to Christmas, aren't you?'

Pod said, 'I'm not talking about Christmas.' That was because his father wouldn't be there.

Cousin Emmy smiled. 'I shall think of you, when we're flying off to the sun. We're going to stay in a super hotel with a swimming pool and a beauty salon, and my mother's going to have a new beach outfit.'

'Splendid,' said Natasha's mummy. 'And will you be able to go to church on Christmas Day?'

'I shouldn't think we'd bother. We'll have so

much else to think about. But I shall have my riding lessons to look forward to, when I come back. Did I tell you I was getting riding lessons for my Christmas present?'

She had. Natasha said, 'Oh, doom and gloom,' quietly to herself. She tried to think about loving your neighbour but somehow it didn't seem to work. Maybe the pool in the super hotel would be full of piranha fish, and they would chew Emmy to pieces as soon as she got into the water. That was a nice thought. Natasha felt enormously cheered, when she thought about piranha fish. Of course, there'd have to be some way of making sure they didn't eat everyone else, as well. Just Cousin Emmy.

'Come along,' said Natasha's mummy, handing out anoraks and scarves. 'I promised we'd go to the Christmas bazaar at the Town Hall this afternoon. It's being run for a children's society so I'll give you a bit extra pocket money to spend as you like, and some for visiting Santa Claus in the grotto.'

'That'll be ace,' said Pod as they walked along. 'I want to ask Santa Claus for something special, about my father.'

'There's no such person as Santa Claus,' said Cousin Emmy, being superior. 'You are silly! Didn't you know it was all a fake? My father told me there are thousands of Santa Clauses all over town, and they're all people who are out of work, and taking a job to dress up as Santa Claus, so as

103

to sell more toys in the shops.'

'It's not always like that,' said Natasha's mummy. 'This Santa Claus certainly isn't doing it for money. You will probably recognise him, if you look closely. It's your old friend the Stilt Man.'

Natasha and Pod exchanged looks. Was Santa Claus a fake?

'You mean,' said Natasha, trying to get to the bottom of the problem, 'that when we write letters to Santa Claus and post them, there's nobody there to take notice?'

'Oh yes, of course,' said Natasha's mummy. 'Parents always take notice, even if they can't always give you exactly what you ask for.'

Pod was silent, stumping along at Natasha's side. Natasha said to him, quietly, 'Did you know?'

He hunched up his shoulders and wouldn't answer. Natasha sighed. She'd suspected the truth last year, but hadn't really known, not for sure and positive. She thought it was much nicer not to have known, really.

They went into the bazaar, but it was so crowded that Natasha's mummy told them to go straight to the grotto and wait there for her. The grotto was decorated with white and silver glitter, and there was a backcloth of a snowy forest scene. Santa Claus sat on a chair, looking big and fat and jolly. He had red cheeks, and a white beard and eyebrows, and a nice chuckling laugh.

Natasha and Pod felt shy. Was it really their old friend the Stilt Man, in a new disguise? And what did they feel about him pretending to be Santa Claus?

Cousin Emmy pushed in front. 'What are you waiting for, stupid? I'm going to ask for something specially nice from his sack.'

There was a big sack on the floor beside Santa Claus, and he gave each child something out of the sack when he'd had a chat with them.

Natasha said to Pod, 'What do you think about going in?'

Pod shook his head. Natasha knew he felt let down, just as she did. They stood to one side, while Emmy sat on Santa's knee. There were lots of other children waiting to see Santa, and they all looked happy about it. Every now and then he would look across at Natasha and Pod, and beckon to them. But they wouldn't go in.

Suddenly there was a lull, and the grotto was empty. Santa Claus got up, and came over to Natasha and Pod.

'Aren't you coming in to have a chat with me?' he said.

'Not now we know you're not real,' said Natasha. 'Sorry, but we don't think it's right, pretending to be Santa Claus, when there's no such person.'

Now they were close up they could see it was indeed the Stilt Man behind the cotton wool and make-up. He said, 'Do you think it's wrong to dress up as the three kings in the nativity play?'

'I don't know,' said Pod. 'I'm one of the kings

105

at school. That is, I would be if I weren't going on strike for Christmas. I'm still thinking about whether I want to be in the play or not.'

'Well, dressing up as Santa Claus is like that. It's remembering what happened.'

'But there's no such person!' said Natasha.

'There was once. A long time ago there was a bishop called Nicholas who went around disguised as an ordinary man, doing good, and giving presents to people who needed them. Especially in the hard winters. Over the years his legend has got mixed up with that of King Wenceslaus. . .'

'Do you mean "Good King Wenceslaus looked out"?' asked Natasha. 'We sing that carol at school, and in church.'

'The very same,' said the Stilt Man. 'And what did he do?'

'He gave things to poor people in the winter-time.'

'That's it,' said the Stilt Man. 'And every winter, people remember him by dressing up as Santa Claus and giving presents to children.'

'Why do we have to give you money, then?'

'I know that in some shops it's just a way of selling toys, but it's different, here. I've collected all these presents from my friends, and I'm giving them away. The money you give me goes towards the children's charity I work for, to help children who are in trouble. I've got two really nice presents for you.'

As he felt around in his sack, Natasha asked,

'What did you give Emmy?'

'A book on fish, I think.'

'Oh, piranha!' thought Natasha, happily. Their friend handed her a marvellous book on grown-up-type trains, and Pod was given a splendid book on birds.

'You won't refuse them, I suppose?' he asked, smiling.

'Oh, no!' said Natasha and Pod together. 'Thank you very much, Santa Claus!'

Pod's Christmas

Pod was having a hard time, trying to ignore Christmas. He had told the teacher at school that he didn't want to be in her nativity play and she hadn't scolded him because she thought he was just being shy. He hadn't made any Christmas cards, but messed around with scissors and paint generally, in the ways boys do sometimes. He hadn't saved up his pocket money – not that he had much – to buy any presents, either.

Natasha had made a whole stack of cards, for her family and her friends, and she'd saved up her pocket money and bought some balls of wool and made brightly coloured woollen pom-poms for everyone. Some of the pom-poms looked a bit wobbly, because Natasha wasn't very good when she first started, but the last ones were really ace.

Natasha was worried about Pod. She knew just how lovely Christmas could be if you thought of it in the right way, but she couldn't really get down to enjoying it if he wasn't enjoying it, too.

She talked to her mummy about Pod and her mummy said that people didn't stop getting ill, or going into hospital, or being sad just because of Christmas. Natasha's mummy said Natasha must pray about it and maybe something marvellous would happen.

Natasha thought her mummy was always telling her to pray about things she couldn't change, and that was all right as far as it went, but when Natasha was worried about something, she wanted to act!

Then something awful happened. Cousin Emmy's father and mother had been planning to take her away with them for Christmas, but at the last minute they had to alter their arrangements for business reasons. Now Emmy's mother and father were going earlier by themselves, and they were sending Emmy to stay with Natasha over Christmas.

Cousin Emmy burst into tears when she heard, and Natasha felt like crying, too.

'It's not fair!' she said to her mummy. 'This is going to be a perfectly horrible Christmas! I wish I hadn't made all those cards and presents! I wish I'd gone on strike for Christmas, like Pod!'

'Hush!' said her mummy. 'You don't really mean that. Be generous, Natasha. Think how awful Emmy must be feeling! We can't refuse to take her in over Christmas, can we? That would be acting like the innkeepers at Bethlehem, so long ago. We can't say "no room at the inn", can we?'

'We've got Pod and his mummy coming, and the old lady from down the road, and that funny man who lives all by himself. Aren't they enough to cope with?'

'I've invited the Stilt Man, and your Aunt Molly and Uncle Tom are coming, too.'

'We'll never get them all round the table,' said Natasha.

'Oh yes, we will. We'll put up an extra table in the sitting-room. It'll be a squash, but who cares? If the people who'd been staying at the inn that first Christmas had squashed up a bit, I dare say there'd have been plenty of room for Mary and Joseph and baby Jesus. Don't you think so?'

Natasha knew when she was beaten. 'Oh, all right. You can let Emmy come, but I wish I could help Pod to be happy about Christmas. He's going to feel awful when I give him his lovely present and he hasn't got anything for me.'

'I've been thinking about that, too,' said her mummy. 'You and Pod have been very good helping me in the kitchen from time to time, and I wonder if you'd like to help him make some fudge to give away for Christmas. We could do it after school tomorrow, if he likes the idea.'

'Yippee!' said Natasha. 'Chocolate fudge?'

'Whatever Pod likes. But I think he ought to provide the ingredients out of his pocket money. I'll give you a list of things for him to buy.'

'Right!' said Natasha. 'Otherwise they wouldn't be his presents, would they?'

She explained this to Pod and he saw the point. 'All right,' he said, 'I don't mind making fudge for everyone, if I've got to. But that's all, OK?'

So after school they made the fudge, and that was good fun. A couple of days later they all went off in the car to fetch the tree. Cousin Emmy came, too, and they were very polite to her, and tried to think about not hurting her feelings when she got stroppy about putting all the best decorations on the tree.

At first Pod didn't want to help decorate the tree, but after a while he got a toadstool and stuck it on the end of a branch and then he helped Natasha's daddy get the lights working, and then he went up the ladder to help with the bits at the top which were hard to reach. Natasha let Emmy put the best ornament of all on the tree. She felt very good inside about this, and her mummy and daddy were pleased with her, too.

'Christmas isn't so bad, is it, Pod?'

'It could have been all right,' said Pod, 'if . . . you know. If my dad had been able to come down.'

When Natasha said her prayers that night, she tried to clean her mind out, ready for Christmas. She hadn't been particularly bad lately, so there wasn't anything she had to say she was sorry for, except. . .

'Please, Jesus, I am sorry about wanting Emmy to be eaten by piranha fish. That was bad of me. But she didn't go away in the end, and the piranhas couldn't get at her, so that's all right. And I will

try to go on being nice to her, though it's an awful strain, and I need some help with that. And please, please, could you help Pod and his mummy to have a nice Christmas, though I don't see how you can do anything about it, really. It doesn't seem that I could really have a happy Christmas, unless Pod was happy, too. Please. Amen.'

Christmas day was extra good. The presents were laid out under the spicy-smelling tree, and the turkey smelt good, cooking gently in the oven, and everyone was smiling and the weather was just right, not too cold, and not too warm. The church was filled with people who all looked happy, and there were decorations on the windowsills and round the crib. Natasha was chosen to take the little clay figure of Jesus right up through the church at the beginning of the service, to put in the crib. As she placed it carefully in the manger, she felt so happy she could have burst.

Even Pod was trying to be happy. He managed a croak or two during the carols and didn't even push back when Emmy shoved past him. They met up with Mrs Pod and all walked back to their house, together with the old lady and the lonely man who were joining them for lunch. Aunt Molly and Uncle Tom had gone to an earlier service and were already at Natasha's house, looking after the turkey.

'Now it's just the Stilt Man we're waiting for,' said Natasha's daddy, looking at his watch. 'I do hope nothing has delayed him.' And he gave

Natasha's mummy a big wink and she laughed, as if being delayed was funny.

'I suppose he's going to dress up as Santa Claus again,' said Emmy. 'I think he's just silly.'

'Here he is!' cried Pod, who'd been looking out of the window. And then Pod went a funny colour, and slid down in the chair.

'What is it?' said Natasha, and scrambled over him to see. The Stilt Man's car had drawn up outside their house. The Stilt Man wasn't dressed up as Santa Claus, but he had a passenger in his car, a big fair-haired man, who looked a bit like him in some ways, but even more like Pod.

'Oh!' cried Pod's mummy, and she ran out of the house, leaving the door wide open. She threw herself into the big man's arms, and he picked her up and hugged her tight.

'It's my dad,' said Pod, quietly. And he said it again, louder. '*It's my dad*!' And then he shouted it. 'IT'S MY DAD, COME HOME FOR CHRISTMAS!'

And he shrieked 'DAD!' and ran out of the house after his mother, and his father picked him up, too, and they all laughed and cried a bit. And then they did some more laughing, till the Stilt Man urged them to get inside out of the cold.

'Well,' said Natasha, 'what I think is, that that's the best Christmas present anyone could possibly have had!'

NATASHA THE BROWNIE

Contents

The talent show

There was to be a talent show in the church hall. Pod and Natasha were such great friends that they decided to do a 'Doctor, Doctor' sketch together, and they practised for weeks to get it just right. Natasha and Pod always meant well, but somehow they were always getting into bother. This time, however, everything was going to be perfect, and everyone would be proud of them.

Natasha's cousin Emmy was going to dance a solo, and her parents had hired a spangly costume for her to wear. As Natasha's mummy took the three children to the concert Emmy said, 'I'm sure to be the star of the show. My dancing teacher said I was a real little performer!'

'Grr!' said Natasha, softly, to Pod.

'Wham, splat!' said Pod back. Which made them

feel a lot better.

Natasha's mummy suddenly stopped and said, 'Oh, I forgot to post these letters. I'll go round by the post-box and meet you at the hall. Surely you can't get into any trouble between there and here. Natasha, drop these magazines into Mrs Dovey's on the way. She was due back from her daughter's last night, and may need something from the shops.'

Off she sent, and while Emmy waited on the pavement, Pod and Natasha turned into Mrs Dovey's gate. But Mrs Dovey didn't reply to their knock, and her curtains were still drawn.

'Hurry up!' cried Emmy. 'You know we won't be allowed to do our turns if we're not there at the start.'

Pod said, 'We could drop the magazines through the letter-box and call in later. Perhaps she's not back yet.'

'I can see a light on in the hall,' said Natasha, 'and I can hear something; maybe she's got the radio on.'

Emmy said, 'Perhaps it's a burglar. Look, I'm going on. I'm not going to risk losing my turn by being late, even if you are.'

Off she went. Pod and Natasha looked at one another. They desperately wanted to go, too, but somehow it just wasn't possible.

'There's someone crying in there,' said Pod. 'Suppose Mrs Dovey's got stuck. She's awfully old and her legs aren't very reliable.'

Pod and Natasha shouted through the letter-box and this time they both heard Mrs Dovey's voice, sounding very weak.

'I've broken my leg! Get the spare key . . . greenhouse!'

Pod and Natasha tore round the side of the house and wrestled the side door open to get into the back garden. What a mess! The grass hadn't been cut for ages, and just about everything you could think of had been dumped on it: plant pots, an old mattress, a broken chair. Beyond was a wreck of a greenhouse, with most of the glass missing.

'Wow!' said Pod, 'What a place for hide and seek!'

Natasha said, 'My dad offered to help her clear it up, but she doesn't like things being disturbed. I bet she fell down the stairs because the stair carpet is loose and she won't let anyone fix it.'

They clambered over the rubbish, and found an old wheelbarrow wedged across the door to the greenhouse. They tried to move it, but it wouldn't budge.

It looked dangerous to climb through a broken window, but they decided it had to be done. They piled enough flower pots together to make something to stand on, and then Natasha pushed, and

Pod heaved himself up . . . and dropped down inside.

The greenhouse was full of piles of newspaper, an old pram, and a jumble of garden tools.

'Where do we start looking?' said Pod in despair.

'Under flower pots,' suggested Natasha, trying to scramble up as well, but finding it rather hard on her hands and clothes.

'Got it!' shouted Pod. He thrust the key up through the broken window to Natasha. Then he had to get out again. He stood on the edge of the pram, and with Natasha pulling, he managed to hoist himself up and out again.

'Phew!' said Natasha, brushing dirt off her hands.

'Ouch!' said Pod, pushing his fingers through a tear in his trousers.

'Oh, well,' said Natasha, swallowing hard, 'We couldn't have got to the concert in time, anyway.'

'Doctor, doctor,' said Pod sadly. 'We need a doctor . . .'

They let themselves in through the front door, and there was Mrs Dovey, lying at the foot of the stairs. It was very cold in the house, but luckily she hadn't taken off her outdoor coat before she slipped and fell. She pointed to the phone, which was in the living-room. Pod dialled for an ambulance, while Natasha fought to light the gas stove and make a cup of tea, just as she sometimes did for her mummy.

The ambulance people told Pod to get some blankets off the bed and keep Mrs Dovey warm. Pod and Natasha did this, and sat with her till the ambulance came. The ambulance men carefully lifted Mrs Dovey into a wheelchair, and were just putting her into the ambulance when Natasha's Aunt Molly came running along the road to look for them.

'Pod! Natasha! Look at you! Oh, you naughty children, what have you been up to? Your mother asked me to come and find you. She's busy doing teas at the hall.'

One of the ambulance men said, 'Now don't you scold them, missus. Proper little heroes they were. Just about saved this lady's life, I reckon!'

'We're very sorry to have missed the concert,' said Pod and Natasha to Aunt Molly as they waved Mrs Dovey off. 'How did Emmy do?'

Aunt Molly looked as if she wanted to smile but didn't think she ought to do so.

'Well, she looked lovely of course, and she started all right, but then she tripped and tore her costume. After that she lost her temper, and didn't finish. Such a pity.'

'Ah,' said Natasha, not quite looking at Pod. She knew he'd be trying not to laugh, too.

They got to the hall as the concert finished, but Aunt Molly marched them on to the stage and told everyone why Pod and Natasha hadn't made it in time.

'And,' concluded Aunt Molly, '*we* were only offering our talents of singing and dancing and telling of stories to entertain you. But these two children were offering their own selves to Jesus, by giving up their chance to shine before an audience, and working to save Mrs Dovey. I think they must have pleased Jesus more than any of us today. So what I say is, three cheers for Pod and Natasha!'

'Oh,' said Natasha, 'How embarrassing!'

The Brownie

Cousin Emmy twirled to show off her brand new Brownie uniform, and said, 'Look at me!' She was wearing a yellow polo shirt and scarf, with brown culottes. Over the shirt she wore a sash.

Natasha's mummy was trying to place a badge on the sash, and said, 'Stand still, Emmy! Natasha, could you do the washing up for me while I do this?'

Natasha sighed, but started on the washing up. Somehow it was always her who got asked to do the washing up, and never Emmy. Life was very unfair at times.

Emmy said, 'I got this badge because of the dancing display, and I'm borrowing my father's stamp collection to show Brown Owl, so's I can get my Collector's badge. I'm going to have lots and lots of badges, more than anyone else in the whole world.'

'Fine,' said Natasha's mummy, 'and I'm sure Natasha will soon catch you up. She's coming along today for the first time, though of course she won't get her uniform till she joins officially.'

Natasha wasn't sure she wanted to join the Brownies. She'd hardly know anyone there, and if they were all like Emmy, it wasn't going to be much fun. Also, she knew Brownies have to keep themselves neat and tidy, and Natasha wasn't good at that.

The only reason she'd agreed to go was that Pod had joined the Beaver Colony which was run by Natasha's daddy, so he wouldn't be around to play with her, and there wasn't much else to do on a Monday night.

So along she went. She walked behind Emmy into the big hall and was introduced by Brown Owl to the other girls in her Six, who were the Pixies. Emmy was a Gnome. Natasha was pleased that she wasn't a Gnome, too. She felt it gave her a better chance, not being in the same Six as Emmy.

The other girls smiled at her, but didn't talk to her much. Natasha felt very much alone. It seemed as if they all had lots of badges.

But then it got better, for they started to play some fun games, and Natasha wasn't bad at games.

She forgot about being shy and really enjoyed herself, especially when her Six came out with top points. That was brill!

If only Emmy hadn't been there, it would have been almost perfect.

Then they made some peppermint creams, and that was absolutely perfect, and Natasha forgot all about Emmy for several minutes. But when she went to the toilet, Natasha overhead Emmy talking to one of the other Brownies.

'Oh, Natasha? She's my cousin. Her people aren't at all well off, you know. She's very untidy, and always getting into trouble. I feel sorry for you girls in her Six. She'll pull you right down.'

Natasha felt herself go bright red with shame. She didn't come out of the toilet until she was sure they'd gone.

She looked in the mirror. Emmy was quite right, she did look a mess. One ribbon was off, and the other untied. She had a smudge on her nose, her T-shirt was hanging out and her socks were at half mast.

She tried to put herself right, but washing only seemed to make the smudge worse, and when she pulled up her socks, one of them produced a hole.

Natasha would have burst into tears, if she'd been that sort of girl. But she wasn't. She was the

sort that soldiers on. But she was so miserable that she did have a little pray to Jesus.

'Please, Jesus, help me. I know I'm untidy, and always getting into trouble because of it. Help me get through the evening, without letting the others down!'

When she went back into the hall she thought she saw the others smiling and talking about her. She pretended she didn't care, but she did, really.

She was so unhappy that it took a real effort to join in with the others at singing time. She could hardly manage to croak through a chorus, even though it was one of her favourites.

She saw her Sixer go up to Brown Owl and say something, looking over at Natasha. Natasha just knew what they were saying, and she wanted to howl with shame. But she didn't. She kept on keeping on, trying to do her best to keep up with the others, and trying not to let them down.

At the end of the evening Natasha waited while some Brownies made arrangements about being tested for badges. Emmy came up, hugging her father's book of stamps. Brown Owl ignored Emmy to smile at Natasha, and ask if she'd enjoyed her first time with them.

'In bits,' said Natasha, 'but please, I won't be coming again. I know I've let the others down, being so untidy. I can't seem to help it. I'm sorry.'

'But, my dear,' said Brown Owl, 'you were just lovely. You helped the Pixies win the games and joined in everything. I know your Sixer is delighted to have you. As for being untidy, well, it's part of the Brownie training to deal with that. For instance, why don't you ask your mother if you can use toggles on your hair, instead of ribbons? I could never manage ribbons myself, when I was your age.'

'Oh,' said Natasha, 'that would be ace! But I don't know that I could ever manage to get any badges. I'm not clever, or anything.'

Brown Owl smiled. 'Well, Natasha, if you do decide to join us, I don't think that would be too much of a problem. Your Aunt Molly is a friend of mine and she's always telling me the nice things you do to help other people. She says you've been helping your mummy ever such a lot with the housework and that means you can work towards the House Orderly badge straight away. Didn't you take part in a play at school last term? That would count towards the Jester badge. And I believe you made a collection of sea shells when you were on holiday, and looked them up in a book, and named them. Bring it to show me some time, and we'll see what else you need to do for the Collector badge.'

'Oh!' said Natasha. 'Really! All those badges for me?'

'You put your talents to work, and you get something to show for it, just as the people did in the Bible. Do you remember? Those who put their talents to work were well and truly rewarded, and the one who didn't, got into a lot of trouble. You don't have to be brilliant at maths or have lots of money to get on, but you do have to make the most of what you've got. Right?'

'Right!' said Natasha.

Brown Owl turned to Emmy and looked through her father's book of stamps. 'I'm sorry, Emmy, but this isn't your collection, is it? I'm afraid I can't start you off on the Collector badge, until you bring me a collection that you've made yourself.'

Emmy was furious, but had to accept what Brown Owl said. Natasha waited for her daddy and Pod, who were coming to collect her after they'd tidied up at Beavers. Pod came out first and said, 'Guess what, Beavers is just ace!'

And Natasha said, 'Guess what! Brownies is brill, too!'

Jericho

Pod had very few toys, and his most treasured possession was his little cat, Jericho. He and his mother lived in a flat above some shops, just down the road from Natasha. Pod's father was away working on an oil rig up north, but when he'd been with them at Christmas, he'd made a cat flap in the back door, so that Jericho could go in and out as he pleased.

Sometimes Natasha and Pod would play hide and seek at the back of the flats, up and down the fire escapes, and round the dustbins and through the overgrown alley. Jericho could hide better than they did, and he always found them when they hid.

But one awful day Jericho refused to come down the fire escape to play. He was shivering. Then he sneezed, and went on sneezing.

Pod and Emmy were having tea at Natasha's house that day. Pod said, making a joke of it, 'Guess what! Jericho's caught a cold!'

Emmy said, 'Silly! Cats can't catch cold.'

Natasha's mummy said, 'I'm afraid they can, Emmy. There is such a thing as cat flu, you know. Perhaps Jericho ought to see the vet. Has he had his flu injection, do you know?'

Pod looked as if he were going to cry. 'I didn't know cats had to have injections. Jericho will be all right, won't he?'

Emmy said, 'He'll probably die.'

Pod rushed from the tea table and hid in the back garden. Natasha found him there, and gave him some biscuits she'd saved from her own tea.

'Perhaps,' said Natasha, 'you could ask your mummy to take him to the vet when she gets back from work tonight.'

When Pod's mummy got back from work, she did take Jericho to the vet, and he told her how to look after him. The vet said Jericho was a very young cat, and seemed to be very poorly, but time would tell.

Pod wasn't sure what that meant, but he saw that his mother looked upset so he gave Jericho an extra cuddle before he went to bed. The next day Jericho wasn't any better, and Pod could hardly wait to get back from school to see how he was.

Natasha went with him. Jericho was curled up in a little ball in his basket and would hardly open his eyes. He did try to purr when Pod stroked him but he hadn't eaten any food that day, or taken any milk.

Pod and Natasha sat with him, silently, hoping for the best. But next morning Jericho wasn't in his basket when Pod went to look.

Pod's mummy sat him on her knee, and said, 'Poor little Jericho. He was feeling so poorly, and now he has gone away from us to get better.'

'I don't understand,' said Pod. 'Where is he?'

'He went to sleep in the night, and didn't wake up this morning. I've put him in a shoe box, out of sight.'

Pod couldn't bear it. He didn't cry, but he wouldn't speak all that day at school. He didn't eat his lunch, either, but just sat there, making Natasha feel guilty for eating hers. She felt like crying, too. She'd loved Jericho almost as much as Pod. It was an awfully long day. Pod tried to excuse himself from going home with Natasha for tea, but Natasha made him come. She felt this was a job for her mummy.

'Listen, Pod,' said her mummy, taking him on her knee. 'This world isn't always perfect. Bad things happen, and sad things happen; like your father having to be away so much, and people and

138

animals dying before we're ready to let them go.'

'You don't understand!' cried Pod. 'It was all my fault. I ought to have known about the flu injections, and done something about it, and then Jericho wouldn't have died!'

'Now you don't know that, and you mustn't blame yourself. It wasn't up to you to think of cat injections. I blame myself a bit. I did know, and I ought to have checked.'

Pod said, 'I can't bear to think of him being gone for ever and ever. At school today Emmy said cats don't ever go to heaven, and I'll never see him again.'

'God made all living creatures,' said Natasha's mummy. 'He knows and cares about even the smallest of sparrows, so of course he knows all about Jericho, who was a lot bigger than a sparrow.'

'Jericho used to catch and eat sparrows,' said Pod. 'I used to tell him not to, but he would do it. Do you suppose Jesus minded?'

'Sparrows were food for him. That was the way he was made. Look to Jesus for comfort, and he will give it to you. Now I suggest that you give Jericho a proper burial in the garden. We'll all come and sing a hymn and pray a bit, and lay him to rest in one of the places where he used to play hide and seek.'

Everyone came to the funeral: Pod's mummy, Aunt Molly and her husband, and Natasha's daddy and mummy. At the last minute Emmy arrived, wearing a black lace scarf over her hair and carrying a beautiful bunch of flowers from the florist's shop. Pod and Natasha were surprised to see Emmy, and even more surprised when she acted just as she should.

They sang 'All things bright and beautiful, All creatures great and small,' and Pod lowered the box containing Jericho into a hole that Natasha's daddy had dug under a flowering bush.

Then Natasha gave a short speech saying what a clever, pretty cat Jericho had been, and how he'd lived life to the full, having to be rescued from trees by firemen, and frightening the lives out of them when he made them think he was a werewolf, and that he'd been the terror of all the sparrows, and they would all miss him a lot.

Natasha's mummy said a prayer thanking Jesus for all the fun they'd had with Jericho, and then they all said the Lord's Prayer, because it felt right. Pod's mummy said something long and complicated in Polish, Pod threw in some earth, and Natasha's daddy filled in the hole.

Then they all went into the house to have a funeral feast of lemonade and cake.

Emmy said, 'That was nice. I had a hamster,

once. It was the prettiest thing, and so soft, you wouldn't believe. It died, and my daddy threw it away in the rubbish. I cried. I really liked that hamster.'

Pod and Natasha looked at Emmy. Perhaps she really was human, after all!

The craft fair

Cousin Emmy boasted, 'We're going to make the most money in the whole world!'

They were preparing for the craft fair, which brought in a lot of money for the church. Everyone was busy making things. Then they would rent a table at the fair and sell what they'd made.

You never saw such beautiful things; there were hand-made sweaters and children's clothes, furry toys, jams and marmalades and pickles, and all kinds of home-made cakes and biscuits.

There were pots and vases and pretty things to hang in windows. There was one stall which sold nothing but furniture and fittings for dolls' houses.

Emmy's parents had booked a stall. They had bought a large quantity of silk flowers cheaply, and proposed to sell them at a profit. Emmy said theirs would be the stall that made the most money at the fair.

Natasha's mummy said, 'What are you going to do at the fair, Natasha?'

Natasha shrugged. She looked at Pod, and he shrugged, too. They couldn't make things to sell. They weren't clever enough, or old enough for that.

Natasha said, 'We'd like to help. Brown Owl did say there would be a way we could help, but I don't know what it is.'

'The Beavers are helping, too,' said Pod, 'because we've been told to wear our uniforms on Saturday.'

'So have the Brownies,' said Natasha.

Emmy said, 'Huh! What can you lot do to help! Not much, I should think. I feel sorry for you. Brown Owl did ask me to help her, but I've something better to do! I'm wearing a new white dress, and I'm going to have a wreath of silk flowers in my hair, and I'm going to help sell the flowers. That's what I call worthwhile helping.'

Natasha and Pod were afraid she was right, but they'd promised, so on Saturday they put on their uniforms and went along to help.

Natasha's daddy was on the door, taking entrance money. He made a big point of letting Natasha and Pod through with the other helpers.

Natasha's mummy went off to help in the kitchens, while Natasha and Pod looked for their leaders. The hall and all the other rooms were filled with big tables, with lots of exciting things on them — puppets and dolls, sweets in every colour and shape. It was hard to keep your eyes off them, and your money in your pocket.

Pod was whisked off by another Beaver, and Natasha found Brown Owl in the room next to the kitchen.

Brown Owl was rushed off her feet. 'I'm glad you've come early, Natasha. We've so much to do. Some of the Brownies are taking teas and coffees round to the stallholders, but we have to make up ploughman's lunches to sell later. We put some of each on a plate, with some salad, and cover it over with clingfilm. Could you help me by cutting up the bread?'

'Is this about right?' said Natasha, cutting away with care.

'Splendid! And here come some more Brownies to help. Isn't Emmy coming, too?'

'She's on a stall already.'

'Oh, well . . . I expect we can manage.'

Natasha cut bread till her forefinger was sore and her arm ached. Another Brownie came to help her. Two more Brownies cut up cheese and butter, while others washed and cut up salad and one filled little pots with chutneys. More Brownies kept coming and going, taking trays with cups of coffee and tea out, and bringing back the empties.

'Phew!' said Natasha, piling the last bits of bread on plates. 'What a marathon that was!'

'Well done!' said Brown Owl. 'Now you can have some orange squash and a biscuit, free. You've worked very hard, and deserve a break. Go and look round all the stalls, but be back in half an hour, when we start to serve lunches.'

Natasha went looking for Pod. There were masses of people at the fair, all talking and buying, and having a good time. There were so many people, it was hard to get round. The stallholders seemed happy, too.

Natasha's daddy was just finishing his stint on the door, and her mummy was sitting with her feet up, having a well-earned cuppa. She had asked a stallholder to put aside a lovely cherry red jumper for Natasha to wear that winter. Natasha was thrilled with the jumper. It was soft and cuddly and had a big black and white panda worked into the front. It was ace.

She hung over the dolls' furniture for a bit because it was so pretty you could just look at it for ever, but she wasn't really a doll person, so she bought some home-made fudge and biscuits at the next stall, to share with her mummy and daddy and with Pod.

But where was Pod? She hadn't seen him anywhere.

She found Emmy's stall, though. It was a picture, with a framework of silk flowers over it. But Emmy herself didn't look happy.

It was most unfortunate, but next door to Emmy's stall was one selling real live flowers, beautifully arranged, and people all seemed to prefer them. Emmy's parents didn't look happy, either. They had sold enough to cover their costs, but not much more.

'Ouch!' Natasha was hit in the back. There was Pod, grinning. He and a Beaver friend were going around with a big plastic bag, picking up all the litter that people dropped. It was the Beavers' task to keep the place tidy, and they were doing a brilliant job.

Then it was time for Natasha and a Brownie friend to help serve the lunches. To and fro they went, offering their ploughman's lunches to the stallholders and to the people who had come to the fair, helping people to chutneys and knives and forks, and taking orders for tea and coffee at the same time.

It was hard to keep track of all the different things that people wanted, so Natasha took the orders down on a piece of paper, while another Brownie collected the money.

They were so busy Natasha didn't notice how

time was passing until Brown Owl said they must sit down and have some lunch. It was only then she saw it was almost time for tea!

'That was very good,' said Brown Owl, smiling as she counted up the money. 'We've made an even bigger profit than last year. Thanks entirely to my helpers! I'm really proud of you, girls!'

Natasha beamed. It had been hard work, but it had been worth it. Pod came and flopped into a chair nearby. He was worn out, too. But he looked equally happy.

'I feel good!' he said. 'I heard someone say that the Beavers and Brownies did as much as anyone to make the craft fair a success!'

'You put yourselves into it,' said Brown Owl. 'That's why.'

The treasure hunt

Natasha's mummy said, 'You remember Mrs Dovey?'

''Course I do,' said Natasha. 'Pod and I helped get her into hospital when she broke her leg.'

'She's decided not to go back to her house, but to live with her daughter instead. Her daughter lives a long way off so Mrs Dovey's asked me to fetch some things that she wants to keep from the old house. Then it can be cleared and put up for sale.'

'Can we help?' asked Natasha.

'Of course. I'll be glad of help, because Mrs Dovey says she's hidden her treasures in different places all over the house, for fear of burglars. The only problem is, she can't remember exactly where she's put everything.'

'Wowee!' said Pod. 'A real live treasure hunt!'

So on Saturday they put on their oldest clothes and went into the empty house.

Even going into that house was an adventure, because it was a Perilous Place to be in. Natasha put her foot through a rotten floorboard, and her leg disappeared, right up to her knee! Luckily she wasn't hurt.

Pod found a waterfall upstairs, where a leaking tap had caused a washbasin to overflow, and the door came off the cupboard under the stairs when Natasha's daddy went there to turn off the water and the electricity.

Natasha said, 'This is more exciting than anything!'

Pod said, 'Do you think there are any wild animals lurking, ready to pounce on us?'

Natasha's daddy ripped up the remains of the stair carpet, so that no-one else could trip and break their leg on it, and they started to search.

Mrs Dovey had given them a list of things she wanted and they soon found three bundles of silver cutlery, and a pearl necklace. But nothing else was where it ought to be!

Pod found a silver tray under the mattress in the spare room, and Natasha cried 'Eureka! More treasure!' when she discovered the silver teapot wrapped in newspaper behind the screen in the fireplace.

Meanwhile Natasha's mummy and daddy collected Mrs Dovey's photograph albums, and the pretty porcelain figures from the sitting-room mantelpiece, and packed up all her clothes.

'Bang, bang!' cried Natasha, peering through a grubby bedroom window. 'Take cover, Pod! There's a wild animal lurking in the jungle outside!'

Pod said, 'Why, it's a cat!' He forced the window open, and called out, 'Here, pussy, pussy!'

The cat darted off, disappearing inside the broken greenhouse.

Pod said, 'Do you think the cat is lost treasure, too?'

Natasha's mummy said, 'If it's grey, it's Mrs Dovey's cat. A neighbour has been feeding it while she's in hospital. But the cat's very unhappy and has been neglecting itself, so the Cat Lady is coming to take it away.'

Pod said, 'What will the Cat Lady do to it?'

'She takes in unwanted cats, and finds new homes for them. Have you found Mrs Dovey's black tin box yet? We can't go till we've found it, because it contains all her private papers.'

But Pod had lost interest in the treasure hunt. He tore out into the back garden, miaowing to the cat.

At first the cat was afraid of him, but Pod was

good with animals, and soon it was purring round his legs. It was a pretty little cat, but it was rather thin and dusty-looking. It was grey all over except for a white chest and paws.

Pod stroked its fur. 'Poor pussy. You're so thin! And you feel so dirty!'

'I expect he's missing Mrs Dovey,' said Natasha. 'I wish we could do something for him.'

'There's plenty of tinned food left out for him, and milk,' said Pod, 'but he doesn't seem to want it.'

'I know what we can do for him!' said Natasha. 'We can give him a shower!'

There was an old watering-can nearby, half full of water. Before Pod could stop her, Natasha had emptied it over the cat! The poor cat didn't like it at all and darted under a tangle of bramble bushes, shivering and crying.

Pod said, 'Oh, come back, pussy!' and tried to scramble after him.

Natasha pulled him back. 'Pod, you'll hurt yourself!'

'What on earth are you doing?' The children turned round to see a nice-looking lady in a sweater and jeans, carrying a cat basket.

'The cat ran away,' said Natasha. 'He was all dirty, so I gave him a shower, but he didn't like

it.'

'I'm afraid it was the wrong thing to do,' said the Cat Lady. 'Cats hate water. Here, kitty . . .'

She put down a bowl full of delicious, freshly cooked fish, and the cat came crawling out on its tummy, and started to sniff at the food. The Cat Lady knelt down and rubbed the cat dry with a towel.

'Oh, let me do that,' said Pod. 'I know he won't mind me. I had a kitten once myself, but he died.'

Natasha said, 'It was my idea to wash it, not Pod's. I'm sorry. I didn't know.'

Pod said, 'If no-one else wants this cat, could I have him?'

The Cat Lady said, 'Let's ask your mummy, shall we? I'd need to know that he would be properly looked after, and given his injections.'

'We know all about that now,' said Pod. 'My mum won't mind. She misses our kitten. She said so only last night.'

'Then I'll have a talk with her, and see what she says. But you must remember that a cat like this, who's been left to run wild, may not want to become a house cat again. He may try to run away, back to this garden.'

'Well, we'd know where to find him, wouldn't we?'

Natasha's daddy gave Mrs Pod's telephone

number to the Cat Lady, who went off to find the phone.

Natasha's daddy said they'd found the tin box of papers in the fridge, and that was the lot. He looked up at the house, and shook his head. 'The house is not going to fetch much. It needs such a lot doing to it. A pity. It's a nice house, underneath.'

The Cat Lady came back and said Pod's mummy was delighted about the cat, and they could have it as soon as it had been checked over by the vet.

'How much money do you want for it?' said Pod. 'You can have everything I've got, only I'm afraid that's not very much.'

'I've got nearly a whole pound that you can have,' said Natasha, 'and I really am sorry about giving it a shower.'

'I don't want anything,' said the Cat Lady. 'I'm just doing God's work, looking after lost animals for him. What will you call him?'

'He has a name already,' said Natasha's mummy. 'He's called Silver because of his silvery-grey coat.'

'What a funny thing,' said Pod. 'We were hunting for silver when we found him.'

Mum's Day

'I've got a problem,' said Pod.

Natasha didn't stop skipping. 'Twenty-one, twenty-two . . . is it your new kitten, Silver?'

'No, he's fine.'

'Twenty-seven, twenty-eight . . . is it your dad?'

Natasha got her skipping rope tangled round her legs. Of course Pod was missing his dad, who hadn't been home for ages. If only he wasn't working so far away! Natasha tried to imagine what it would be like if her dad had to work so far away, and decided it didn't bear thinking about.

'It's not dad. It's my mum.'

'What about your mum? She's all right, isn't she?'

'It's Mothering Sunday coming up. I've made her a card and I want to give her a present, but I haven't got any money. I've thought till I'm tired, and I still can't think how to get her a present.'

'I haven't got a present for my mum, either. This calls for a Confabulation.'

Natasha liked big words. She saved them up for special occasions, when they might come in handy. Pod looked impressed when she used her new word, so she explained it meant a discussion, and they sat down under a tree in the playground to talk it over.

Natasha said, 'I made my mum a card, too. Only it went a bit wrong. My writing went so big I had to put 'Mum's Day' on it, instead of Mothering Sunday. I don't think she'll mind. I wanted to make her a nice present, too. I tried to make a plant pot holder with string, but it broke.'

'I tried to get some money, washing cars. But they said I was too little.'

'Cousin Emmy's buying her mother a bottle of scent, the new one that's on the telly adverts. She gets so much pocket money, she can easily afford it.'

'Yuk,' said Pod.

'Absolutely yuk,' said Natasha. 'Wow! I've just had an idea. You know our teacher was telling us about a special cake for Mothering Sunday? Girls who worked away from home used to take a simnel cake to their mothers when they went back to see

157

them at this time of year. The teacher said some people believed the cake was called after a boy called Sim and a girl called Nell. Just like you and me, only different names.'

'That's right,' said Pod. 'Sim and Nell had an argument about whether the cake should be boiled or baked. So they did both, and named it after both of them, Sim-Nel cake. So what!'

'So why don't we make our mums a simnel cake?'

'Wouldn't it be too hard?'

'I've done some cooking at Brownies, and you're good at measuring. I bet we could do it, if we tried. What I think is, that we get permission for you and Silver to stay with us on Saturday night. We get up early on Mothering Sunday, and do it in our kitchen. Then it will be a lovely surprise for them.'

'You're on!' said Pod.

Their mothers agreed to Pod and Silver staying the night at Natasha's, so the first part of their plan went off very well.

Early on Sunday morning Pod and Natasha got out of bed and crept downstairs.

Pod had got properly dressed even though it was so early. While he fed Silver, Natasha tied a big apron of her mum's over her pyjamas and pushed her hair into her Brownie hat to keep it out of the way.

First they got down the big cookery book from

the shelf. Pod read off the list of things they needed while Natasha got them from the larder. They found everything except the marzipan, so they decided to do without that.

Pod rolled up his sleeves and measured everything out onto the table in piles. Natasha put the oven on to warm, found the baking tin, and started to crack eggs into a bowl.

Then disaster struck. Silver jumped up onto the table and accidentally knocked over half a bottle of milk. The milk went all over the table and got mixed up with the flour and the sugar and the currants.

'Mop it up, quickly!' shrieked Natasha.

'Can't you see I'm trying to hold it back with my hands?' shouted Pod. 'Get a cloth!'

'I can't! I'm cracking eggs . . .'

'It's going over the edge of the table . . .'

'Ouch! It's going down my tummy!'

Natasha hopped around, holding an egg in each hand, with the milk trickling down her pyjamas. Poor Silver was so alarmed at what he'd done that he dived off the table under Natasha's feet.

Pod shouted 'Look out!' but Natasha slipped and fell, bringing down the towel rail and knocking over the stack of pots and pans in the corner.

When the noise had died down, they remembered the grown-ups, and looked up at the ceiling.

Surely Natasha's father and mother must have heard them!

Nothing happened.

'It's all right,' whispered Natasha. 'I bumped myself really hard, but I didn't break the eggs!'

'Great!' whispered Pod back. 'And no-one heard us!'

And at that very moment Natasha's daddy walked in, pulling on his dressing-gown. 'What's going on here?' he said, and groaned when he saw the mess.

'Sorry,' said Natasha. 'We'll clean it up, honest. We were making a surprise present for mum . . .'

'A simnel cake,' said Pod. 'Only it got a bit complicated.'

'I can see that!' said Natasha's daddy. 'Well, if it's for Mothering Sunday, perhaps I'd better lend a hand.'

So Natasha's daddy showed them how to use the electric mixer which made cooking easy.

He said simnel cakes had to have marzipan, which was what made them different from other fruit cakes. So he looked up the recipe and helped them to make their own.

Then Pod spooned half the cake mixture into the baking tin, Natasha's daddy put in a layer of marzipan, and Natasha dolloped on the rest of the mixture, smoothing it off to go in the oven.

While the cake was baking, Pod and Natasha made twelve little balls of marzipan to go round the top of the cake – to remind them of the twelve apostles – and Natasha's daddy found some miniature sugar eggs to go in the middle, to show that Easter was coming.

Natasha's mummy came down before they had time to clean up the kitchen and she was a bit upset about the mess at first. But when she saw the cake she was thrilled, and agreed that of course you couldn't cook a surprise cake without making a mess. They cut the cake in two, and Natasha's mummy found a cake box for Pod to take half back home.

As for Pod's mummy, she said Pod had given her not one but two gifts for Mothering Sunday, the best cake she had ever tasted, and a Good Rest!

The Easter egg

Cousin Emmy took the last chocolate biscuit and said, 'What are you getting for Easter?'

'Getting?' said Natasha, puzzled. 'You mean presents? It's not Christmas or birthday.'

Natasha's mummy found another chocolate biscuit each for Pod and Natasha, and said, 'It's better than Christmas. Without Easter, we wouldn't have anything to be joyful about.'

Pod said, 'Mega-thanks for the biscuit.'

Emmy said, 'I'm getting my hair done, and a new dress, and of course the biggest Easter egg you ever did see.'

Pod and Natasha weren't interested in hair-dos or new clothes, but their eyes did shine at the thought of Easter eggs.

Natasha's mummy said, 'Yes, you will have one

163

each, though I don't think they'll be very big, because we're having so many people to lunch that day. Aunt Molly and Uncle Tom, and your old friend the Stilt Man, who works for children's charities, and . . .'

'And me and Mum?' enquired Pod. 'I did hope we'd go up north to be with Dad for Easter, but Mum says we have to stay here.'

'Of course you're coming,' said Natasha's mummy. 'And perhaps Emmy as well.'

'I should think not!' said Emmy. 'We're all flying to Tenerife for Easter.'

Pod and Natasha knew that Emmy's ideas of going away with her parents didn't always work out. They hoped she would go. They also hoped they'd be nice to her if she didn't. It put a strain on them, being nice to Emmy.

When Emmy had gone home, Natasha asked her mummy if she could have a chocolate egg with buttons in it, as this was her favourite.

'I hadn't forgotten,' said her mummy.

'And Pod?'

'I'll check with his mum and make sure he gets one. And Natasha, try to be kind to Emmy.'

'I do *try*,' said Natasha.

'I must warn you that Emmy's parents probably won't be taking her away with them. I expect they'll spend a great deal of money on presents for her instead.'

'You mean she really is getting a giant Easter egg?'

'Yes. Let's hope she remembers why we have eggs at Easter time. You remember why, don't you Natasha?'

Natasha nodded, though she didn't, not really. It was just something nice that happened at Easter time, like decorating the church with daffodils and all the other yellow flowers they could find, and singing really happy hymns that made you want to clap your hands.

She liked everything about Easter, and even managed to keep smiling when she heard that Emmy would not be going to Tenerife, and would be staying with them, instead. Natasha succeeded in being nice to Emmy right up to Easter morning when Pod rushed round before church to show them his very own chocolate egg. Natasha showed him hers, and everything was lovely until Emmy unpacked the one her parents had left for her.

Emmy's egg was so big she could hardly see over it! It made Pod and Natasha's normal-sized eggs look tiny. Pod and Natasha said, politely, how beautiful Emmy's egg was, and would she like to taste a piece of theirs.

Emmy accepted the pieces they offered her, and said, 'Don't you think this is the biggest and the best Easter egg there ever was? I'd rather have this than go to Tenerife. Don't you think it's super, Natasha?'

'Marvellous,' said Natasha, being generous about it. It did look marvellous, too. There were flowers on it, and fluffly nylon chickens and an enormous bow of yellow ribbon. Natasha thought there was enough chocolate in it for a whole family.

Emmy said, 'Don't you think it's splendid, Pod?'

'Wow!' said Pod, impressed. 'Can we have a bit of yours now?'

Emmy shook her newly-permed head. 'It's not for you. It's for me. All for me.'

The injustice of this bit deep into Natasha and Pod. They looked round for a grown-up to even things up, but all the grown-ups were either in the kitchen, or getting ready to go to church.

'Bother her!' said Pod to Natasha as they walked along.

'Hope it makes her sick!' said Natasha to Pod. And they continued to feel cross till they got to church.

It was lovely at church, with flowers and everyone being happy and having so much to celebrate. Pod and Natasha even managed to overlook the fact that Emmy had brought her egg to church for the other children to admire. Easter was too special to waste time on being jealous of other people's eggs.

The minister told all the children to come up to collect a chocolate egg from a big basket. He explained that eggs were the sign of new life, to remind us of the new life that started on the first Easter day when Jesus rose from the dead. He said an egg was also the symbol of the stone which had been rolled away from the empty tomb. All the children took an egg, and then they had to roll them down the aisle to see who reached the door first.

Off they went, rolling the eggs along. The eggs went all over the place, and the grown-ups started laughing. Everyone was laughing and happy, and Pod was the happiest of all when he got his egg to the door first, and was given an extra Easter egg as a prize.

Everyone thought it was a splendid way of remembering what happened on the morning when Jesus rose from the dead.

Even then the children didn't go straight back to their seats, but crowded round the minister as he showed them the Easter garden which Natasha's class had made, with the tomb all empty, and lit up with a pocket torch from inside. They sang Allelulias and clapped in time to the music, and only then did they go back to their seats for the final blessing.

But Natasha noticed that Emmy went bright red during the last prayer, and looked as if she were going to cry.

Emmy had accidentally sat down on her beautiful Easter egg and mashed it into dozens of pieces, which clung to her new dress when she stood up again.

Poor Emmy. Everyone made a fuss over her, and took her away to be cleaned up.

Pod said to Natasha, 'That's odd. If you'd told me it was going to happen, I'd have thought that I'd have laughed myself silly. But somehow, I don't want to laugh, now.'

'We've got friends and lots of people who like us,' said Natasha. 'She only had her egg.'

Pod said. 'Shall I give her the one I got for a prize?'

'She doesn't deserve it.'

'I know that,' said Pod. But he gave it to her, all the same.

Great Pa, ta

Easter had come and gone. One day more and they would be back at school. At church on Sunday Pod slumped in the pew, and refused to take part in the service. He wouldn't stand up to sing the hymns, he wouldn't put his hands together and bow his head when it came to prayers, and he kicked the front of the pew all through the minister's talk to the children.

After church Natasha asked Pod what was the matter.

Pod kicked the floor, and didn't reply.

'Is it your dad! Has something happened?'

Pod shook his head. 'I thought he'd be coming down to visit us for Easter, since we couldn't go up there. I thought it would be a nice surprise, like it was at Christmas. I haven't seen him since

Christmas.'

Natasha said, 'We could have a special pray about it.'

'It's no good. Do you think I haven't been praying, all this time? And that silly minister, going on about how much we've got to be thankful for, and telling us to make up our own prayers, like "Great Pa, ta!" '

Natasha said, 'But I liked that. It was, well, friendly. It made me feel closer to him.'

Pod hunched his shoulders. 'It was yuk. It made me feel sick.'

The minister had been comparing the lives of most children in Britain with those of the starving children in certain parts of Africa. Pod knew why the minister had told them to be thankful, but he just couldn't do it.

He was feeling sick at heart, just as sick as those poor children were, though in a different way.

'I'll tell you what I think,' said Pod. 'I've had enough of church and praying. It doesn't work. I'm not coming any more.'

Natasha went pale. She couldn't imagine coming to church without Pod. It would be awful. As she watched Pod trudge off all by himself, she heard the rustle of Cousin Emmy's new dress.

'Well!' said Cousin Emmy. 'Didn't Pod behave badly in church! Everyone's talking about it.'

Natasha felt like crying. 'He's upset about his dad not coming home at Easter.'

'I expect they're having a divorce,' said Cousin Emmy, casually. 'That's what happens, when people live apart. My mother and father have talked about it quite a lot.'

Natasha was shocked. 'But Emmy, that's awful! Aren't you upset?'

Emmy shrugged. 'So I get two homes and two lots of presents at Christmas and birthdays. So what?'

Natasha went to find her mummy and tell her what Emmy had said. 'Pod's father and mother aren't going to get a divorce, are they? I think he'd die if they did.'

'Oh, my dear, no! Of course not! Mr Pod couldn't get down for Easter because ... well, there was a special reason, and you'll know all about it soon enough.'

'But Emmy said ...'

'That's an entirely different matter. Emmy's parents are going through a rough time, and we must all pray for them.'

'I'm not praying for Emmy. She doesn't mind if they do get a divorce.'

'Emmy puts a brave face on it, but I'm sure she's very upset inside.'

Natasha wasn't so sure about that, but for the

moment she was more concerned about Pod.

'Pod says he's stopped praying, and won't come to church any more. I don't know what to do. I don't want to come to church either, if he doesn't!'

'Darling, you're not thinking straight. You believe Jesus loves you? And Pod? Remember that Jesus knows what's best for you and he loves you very much. He doesn't promise that everything will turn out exactly as you want it to in this world. But in this case . . . well, I wouldn't give up hope, and that's all I can say for the moment.'

'I'm fed up with secrets, and so is Pod. Every time he asks his mum about his dad, she gets cross and says she'll tell him when there's any news.'

Natasha's mummy sighed. 'Yes, it's very trying, waiting . . . but we've all got to be patient.'

That night Natasha had a nightmare about Pod's father getting in a boat and going away for good. She woke up crying, and was inclined to be cross with everyone next day. To make matters worse, Pod wouldn't talk to her, or answer when the teacher spoke to him. He even refused to play at break-time.

Natasha was afraid he'd get into serious trouble if he went on like that, so she dragged him aside into the corner under the beech tree.

He wouldn't even look at her, so she put her hands on her hips and said, 'Pod, you can't stop hoping. I won't let you! Let's have a pray about it, here and now. If it doesn't bring your dad back, at least it will make us feel better!'

'Won't!' said Pod.

'Then I will, and I shall hang on to you, so that you can feel my prayer, even if you're too stupid to pray for yourself!'

She shut her eyes tight, and prayed as hard as she could. She could feel Pod trying to pull away from her, but she didn't let go, and went on praying.

When she stopped and opened her eyes, he was still looking down, but he didn't look as awful as before.

'Better?' said Natasha. Pod nodded.

And that very same evening while Pod was having tea at Natasha's, there was a phone call which Natasha's mummy took out in the hall.

'Marvellous news!' said Natasha's mummy, rushing back into the room with a great big grin on her face. 'Pod, that was your mother on the phone. Your dad's just rung her at work to say he's landed the job he's been after, the one down here, in London! And what's more, Mrs Dovey has agreed to sell him her old house!'

Pod couldn't take it in. He sat there with a chocolate biscuit in one hand and his mouth open. He didn't even blink, he was so surprised.

Natasha's mummy said, 'No-one dared say anything in case it all fell through. Your father's been trying and trying to get a job down here. He kept getting short-listed and not getting the job, but now he has, and you can all be together again. And in your very own house, too!'

Still Pod stared ahead, and didn't speak.

Natasha said 'Wow! What fantastical good news!' She nudged Pod. 'You know another good thing? Your kitten Silver will be able to go back to his old home to live.'

Pod shifted his eyes to Natasha, and back to her mum. He still didn't speak.

'Come, on Pod!' said Natasha. 'Say something!'

Pod put his hands together, closed his eyes, and said, 'Great Pa, ta!'